T
MYSTERIOUS
CASE

D0462000

Dave Gustaveson

YWAM
Publishing
A Ministry of Youth With A Mission
P.O. Box 55787, Seattle, WA 98155
(206) 771-1153

The Mysterious Case
Copyright © 1995 by David Gustaveson

Published by Youth With A Mission Publishing
P.O. Box 55787
Seattle, WA 98155 USA

ISBN 0-927545-78-0

Printed in the United States of America

To those
who sacrifice
themselves to help the
hundred million street kids
in the world today.

Other

REEL KIDS
Adventures

The Missing Video
Mystery at Smokey Mountain
The Stolen Necklace
The Mysterious Case
The Amazon Stranger
The Dangerous Voyge

Available at your local Christian bookstore or
YWAM Publishing
1(800)922-2143

Acknowledgments

When I discovered that countless millions of street children are exploited everyday in factories and fields worldwide, I needed a way to somehow communicate this to others. Hence this book.

Throughout India, children as young as five toil their youth away in the blacklisted industries, working 12 to 16 hours a day under terrible conditions that even the hardiest adults would find sickening.

Today, the enemy is not just attacking children, but childhood. City streets are both the stage and battlefield for children of the poor and needy. Many of the kids are there because of breakdowns in family structure, poverty, physical and sexual abuse, parental exploitation, armed conflicts and wars, famine, and so on.

Something must be done. I trust every kid reading this book will not only enjoy the adventure, but be touched in their hearts to get involved.

A number of people offered help on the research for this book. First of all, I want to thank Jeannette Lakasse for her tremendous insights on the street kids. Kids' work in Belo Horizonte is changing lots of kids lives.

Also to Jimmy Reysen for his timely help. Special thanks to Tom and Terri Bragg, Jim and Michelle Drake, and Warren Walsh. Their tireless work at YWAM Publishing will be forever rewarded.

Also thanks to my wonderful editor, Shirley Walston. It is always a joy working with her. She adds polish.

And of course, to my wife Debbie and my two daughters, Jamie and Katie for keeping me encouraged.

And special thanks to the dedicated workers in Youth With A Mission and other organizations like World Vision who minister to street kids daily around the world. You are a blessing, and will see your reward now and forever.

Table of Contents

Chapter 1

Bad Mistake

Oh, no!"

At first, Jeff Caldwell barely heard the faint cry. He cocked his head and listened closely.

"Oh, no!"

The voice was louder this time. Unmistakable. It was his sister Mindy.

The 15-year-old ran his fingers through his short blonde hair, shook his head, and strained to listen. He was beginning to regret his decision to stay with his sister while she unpacked. It was early evening, and he and the rest of the Reel Kids Club had just landed in Bogota, the capital of Colombia. The others had gone on a walk to explore the city. And until now, everything had been perfect.

When he heard a thud against the wall, he knew he couldn't wait any longer. He hurried next door, his blue eyes alert to anything amiss in the hallway.

He tapped on Mindy's door and as he opened it, he saw his sister pacing across the room. When she got to the wall, she gave it a whack with the toe of her tennis shoe, reversed her direction, and continued pacing. With every step, she glared at the burgundy suitcase that lay sprawled open across the bed.

Mindy's eyes were red from crying, and she had tossed her brown-rimmed glasses on the dresser. She tugged fiercely at her blonde ponytail—something she always did when she was upset—then looked up at him pathetically.

"What's wrong, Min?" Jeff cautiously asked.

Angry tears dribbled down her flushed cheeks. "He got the wrong one," she groaned.

Jeff stood for a moment, confused. Then he moved closer. "Who got the wrong what?"

"K.J."

Jeff wondered what his best friend had to do with it. "What did he do?"

"Got the wrong suitcase." A hint of anger edged her voice. "Look at this stuff! This suitcase isn't mine! Now I'll have nothing to wear."

Jeff studied the burgundy suitcase. It looked exactly the same as the one Mindy had received as a Christmas gift. Cardboard dividers covered everything inside. He peeked under one side and couldn't believe his eyes.

The silky fabrics didn't look at all like Mindy's usual jeans and sweaters. The clothes looked like they'd come straight from the most expensive shops on Rodeo Drive in Beverly Hills. He lifted a ruffled pink blouse and a lacy dress to uncover jars and bottles of expensive-looking cosmetics.

"Hmmm. This is new," he said, holding the blouse up against his chest. "Maybe Mom threw it in to surprise you."

"Come on, Jeff! I'm serious." Mindy smacked him on the arm.

"Okay, okay." Jeff couldn't help but laugh.

"I'm going to kill K.J. when he gets back," Mindy fumed. "He always does this kind of stuff."

"Why do you always think everything is his fault?"

"Simple. The dummy offered to get my suitcase at the airport, but he didn't even look at the name tag. From now on, I'll carry it myself." Mindy sighed as she headed to the bathroom.

Jeff sat on the wooden chair near the bed. He felt bad for Mindy, but he knew that a phone call to the airport's baggage department would probably solve everything. He also knew he had to give her a minute before suggesting it.

He anxiously tapped his foot. He badly wanted to get outside and explore the city. The snow-capped splendor of the mountains surrounding Bogota seemed to call to him.

Jeff recalled the information Mindy had shared about Bogota. As she did before each of the Reel Kids trips, she had researched the country and its people. She said Colombians were known to be some of the most charming human beings in the world. Jeff couldn't wait to experience for himself the culture and history of the old Indian town.

Since he'd heard about this mission trip, he had crossed off the squares on his calendar while waiting for this day—Thursday, December 26. He and the Reel Kids Club had come to Bogota to make a video featuring International Children's Centers, an agency that helped *gamines*, or kids who lived on the streets.

Jeff and Mindy's dad worked as an anchorman on a local television station. He had already arranged for the Reel Kids video to be aired in late January on a national news program. Hopefully, it would raise money to help with the important work to street kids.

Jeff, Mindy, and Jeff's best friend, K.J., had joined the Reel Kids Club after they had moved to Los Angeles. Their leader, Warren Russell, headed the Communications Department at their high school. Though the club met off campus, they were still able to use school equipment. After every trip, they produced videos to inspire others into missions work.

Through the club, Jeff, Mindy, and K.J. had been to parts of the world most kids never see, perhaps never knew existed. They had worked in Cuban churches, had helped the 20,000 people who live at Smokey Mountain, a city dump in the Philippines, and had stopped an ivory smuggling ring in Kenya. The videos they showed in churches and youth groups educated and inspired people to make a difference in others' lives.

Jeff knew that playing their video about Colombia on prime time television was an incredible opportunity to show thousands of people about the plight of Bogota's street kids. He was anxious to help in any way he could.

But at this moment, he realized Mindy wouldn't survive without her clothes. Calling the airline baggage department was the obvious solution, but he needed their host, Ricardo, to translate. The call would have to wait until the others came back from their walk.

He didn't look forward to K.J.'s return. It would surely mean war—a big war—with Mindy.

Jeff took a deep breath when he heard whistling noises coming from the living room. He peeked down the hall. Sure enough, it was his 14-year-old buddy, K.J.

Kyle James Baxter, alias K.J., had mischievous dark eyes and a thick crop of carefully combed black hair. He always bounced in his tennis shoes, displaying the energy moving in his wiry 5' 6" frame. Jeff admired his best friend's passion for life, but he also knew how crazy and impulsive K.J. could be.

Mindy opened the bathroom door, and Jeff could tell by the look on her face that she'd heard the whistling too. She was a volcano preparing to explode, and it was too late to stop her now.

K.J. strutted into the room. "You guys wouldn't believe how beautiful the city is tonight," he said with his usual charming smile. "But it's hard to breathe at 8,600 feet."

Jeff rocked back and forth on his heels and tried to smile.

Mindy dried her face on a towel as she walked out of the bathroom. When she got close enough, she tossed it at K.J.

"K.J.," she said through clenched teeth, "I wouldn't worry about the altitude. You're not going to be breathing long."

Jeff stepped over to stand between them. He and K.J. had been best friends since the fourth grade. K.J. had lived with his mom since his parents' divorce, but he spent a lot of time with the Caldwells. He was almost like a brother to Mindy— at least they fought like siblings.

"Wait a minute, Mindy," Jeff said, using his hands to keep them apart. "Let's hear his story."

"What did I do now?" K.J. asked, taking a giant step backward.

"You messed up, K.J.!" Mindy yelled. "Real bad this time."

Jeff pushed a chair over for K.J. to sit in. He quickly explained the suitcase problem. K.J. reached for the identification tag, and his face turned pale.

"Rosa Alvarez? Do we know a Rosa Alvarez?" K.J. asked weakly.

"Good question," Mindy snapped.

"Look, Mindy. I'm sorry. I was just trying to help," K.J. protested.

"Don't do me any more favors. Just like the suit-case, most of my stuff was Christmas gifts—a new dress, jeans, blouses, shoes, CDs. And then there were my research papers on Bogota and all my com-puter stuff!"

K.J. lifted the cardboard dividers, running his hands through the clothes, avoiding Mindy's deadly stares. "Wow, Mindy, I think you got a better deal." As usual, K.J. tried to joke his way out of the predicament. "There's some pretty great stuff here. It would make you look like a real girl."

Mindy raised her fist to punch K.J., but Jeff moved in fast.

"Cool it," Jeff ordered. "That's not funny."

"Okay, so what's the big deal?" K.J. asked, exasperated. "I'm sorry, all right? Let's report the mistake to Avianca airlines. I'm sure Rosa wants her stuff back too."

Jeff looked at his watch. It was 6:30 p.m. "We have to wait for Warren and Ricardo to get back. We don't speak Spanish, remember? Do you know where they went?"

K.J. nodded. "They're on the main street where I was. Ricardo was showing Warren the street kids' center. They said they'd be back before eight."

"What do we do now?" Mindy asked, turning away from K.J.

Jeff scratched his curly head. "We'll have to wait. I'm sure Avianca's baggage department will stay open until then."

The room grew silent. Jeff knew how tired and frustrated Mindy was, but he also knew sitting and thinking about it wasn't going to help matters. After a few minutes, he snapped his fingers.

"Let's not just sit here and be depressed," he said. "Let's go for a walk before it gets dark."

"I'm not going anywhere with him," Mindy sizzled.

As the appointed leader when Warren was gone, Jeff knew he needed to maintain peace. "K.J., why don't you just give us a few directions so Mindy and I can go?" he suggested. "She'll feel better with some fresh air."

"I certainly hope so," K.J. grumbled. "I need to unpack anyway."

"Look, Jeff," Mindy turned toward him as they walked, "I know I'll get my suitcase back. I just wish K.J. would use his brain once in a while."

Jeff laughed a little. "Try to forget it for now, Mindy. Let's enjoy Bogota."

The cool mountain air felt refreshing as they headed down a main street called Carrera 15. Although it was Christmastime, Bogota's summer was just beginning. The mountain town had a reputation for its perpetual springlike climate.

Jeff inhaled deeply. "I feel a little dizzy."

"It's the altitude. They say it takes a couple of days to adjust to the thin air."

Jeff knew Mindy was happiest when she was sharing the knowledge she'd acquired in her studies.

"I had so much fun researching for this trip," Mindy continued. "I read that Bogota is called 'the city of fire and ice.' It is located 8,700 feet up in the Andes, yet it's only a few degrees from the equator."

"City of fire and ice?"

"The sun shines so fiercely it almost crackles," Mindy explained, "while cold rains blow in over the mountains. The temperature is never much above 58 degrees."

"You always do such great research."

"Thanks." She gave him a smile. "Bogota was fun. There are so many writers here. And poets. They say more poets than generals become president of Colombia. And the place has so much to see."

Then Mindy frowned. "I love my job as researcher for the club. And that's why I'm so mad. Most of my paperwork is in the suitcase."

Jeff nodded, but he knew that even without her notes and computer, Mindy still remembered more than he'd probably ever know.

He looked up at the incredible sunset that was quickly forming over the Andes. The steep mountains loomed darkly against the vast sky. A cold, misty wind blew a few raindrops into his face, reminding him again that they were in a different climate from their home in Los Angeles.

Mindy held up her hands to catch the raindrops. "I've heard the only thing you can be sure of about Bogota is that you can never be sure about the weather."

Walking further down the street, Jeff couldn't take his gaze away from the towering mountains. They were a huge presence above the street. He spotted a great white church on a distant mountain.

"What's that?" he asked, pointing to it.

"We need to get some footage of that," Mindy replied. "It's one of the most famous places here in Bogota, on the summit of a mountain called Monserrate."

Jeff still felt like he couldn't get enough air. Breathing deeply, he smelled the beautiful flowers from the lush gardens that surrounded them—orchids, bougainvillaea, roses, and hibiscus.

He noticed the patched tin shacks surrounding the wealthy city. He figured they had to be the homes of the poor. Mindy told him that in those shacks some lived three families to a room. The sight made Jeff sad.

Looking at his watch, he noticed it was 7:30. "We better get back to the house now."

They quickly retraced their steps. Turning the last corner, Jeff recognized the large one-story house where they were staying. The house had been donated to International Children's Centers, ICC, to serve as their headquarters. The ministry operated several centers for street kids around the city.

Their host, Ricardo, and a few staff members lived in the bedrooms that weren't used as offices. When groups like the Reel Kids came to help, they stayed at the house as well. Jeff felt lucky to be living with people who had dedicated their lives to saving street kids.

The house had white adobe walls and windows decorated with red grillwork. Under the eaves of the tile roof was a twelve-by-fifteen-foot veranda furnished with simple wooden tables and chairs.

"When we arrived earlier, I didn't even notice this beautiful stained glass," Jeff said as they stepped onto the small porch.

He stood back and stared at two stained glass angels. They stood six feet tall, one on each side of the front entrance. One was blowing a trumpet and the other was strumming a harp.

"With the hall light shining behind them, they

almost look real, don't they?" Mindy added quietly. "Like they're standing guard over the house. They make me feel safe."

As Jeff and Mindy entered the hallway which connected the eight bedrooms to the living and dining area, they heard familiar voices.

Jeff immediately spotted Warren. Warren was an inch taller than Jeff, but they had the same medium build. His sandy brown hair was cropped short enough for him to have joined the army with no need for a haircut. His soft brown eyes always radiated friendliness and warmth. He was dressed in dark blue slacks and a sweater to match. Though he was in his early thirties, he looked young enough to be a student. The team called him "Warren" on trips, but always "Mr. Russell" when they were at school. His deep love for God and compassion for people were obvious. Jeff knew he enjoyed every minute of these Reel Kids trips.

Jeff then glanced at their Colombian host, Ricardo. His tender and teary dark eyes spoke of the love he had for his work with Bogota's street kids. Jeff guessed he was almost the same age as Warren. Ricardo was about 5' 10" and athletic, and he had enough jet black hair for two heads. Mindy had described him as dashing, and she had asked Jeff why he was single. Ricardo was dressed in a neatly pressed white shirt and black slacks. His conservative tie peeked above the neck of a red sweater.

Upon entering the room, Jeff noticed a shorter man talking quietly with Ricardo. His hair still showed the teeth marks from the comb he'd used to slick it back. He wore a business suit, but he looked comfortable—as if he wore one every day.

"Hi," Warren greeted Jeff, then he placed a comforting arm around Mindy's shoulder. "You okay? Seems like we always have some kind of challenge on these trips. Sorry about your suitcase. We've tried to call Avianca."

"I'm fine," Mindy said. "But I'd really love to get out of these same old jeans. Did they find my suitcase?"

"We keep getting Avianca's answering machine," Ricardo replied, walking toward them. "I'll keep trying."

K.J. bounded into the room like a puppy then stopped short. Warren chuckled as K.J. did a double take when he realized they had company.

Warren smiled. "Let me introduce you to Franco."

Franco's business-like appearance made the team act formally at first. But as he shook their hands, he flashed a huge smile and spoke to them in near-perfect English. That put everyone at ease.

"Franco is a pilot," Warren said. "He lives a few miles from here and flies Ricardo around Colombia and other parts of Latin America. He may take you on a plane ride in the next few days."

"Really?" K.J. exclaimed. "That would be awesome!"

"Why don't you relax for a while?" Ricardo said, excusing himself. "I'll worry about the suitcase."

The team peppered Franco with questions for nearly an hour before he had to get home to his family.

Jeff looked at his watch. It was 9:30. He had dozed off in a chair. Rubbing his eyes, he looked around at the empty living room then headed to the kitchen. Ricardo and Warren were sitting at the table, staring at the suitcase. The looks on their faces worried him.

"Did you find Mindy's suitcase?" Jeff asked.

Both turned to Jeff with a cold stare.

"What's wrong?"

Warren motioned for Jeff to sit down. "I know you're not going to believe this, but Franco just called from his house."

Looking at their faces, Jeff wasn't sure he wanted to hear any more.

"He heard on the radio that two members of the drug cartel were arrested at the airport today," Warren continued.

"So?" Jeff asked. "What's that got to do with us?"

"They were on the same Avianca flight as we were." Warren's eyes filled with concern. "The radio reported that one of their suitcases is missing, and the police are searching for it."

Chapter 2

Street Kids

Jeff's eyes widened. "Do you think this is the one they're looking for?" He pointed at the suitcase on the table.

Ricardo looked at the name tag. "Maybe."

"What are we going to do?" Jeff asked, looking from Warren to Ricardo.

"Nothing tonight," Ricardo said. "We'll wait 'til morning. Then we'll go to the police."

"Man, we don't want to get involved with a drug cartel," Jeff commented quietly. "They're dangerous."

Ricardo nodded, stroking his mustache. For a moment, no one spoke.

"Does Mindy know about this?" Jeff finally asked.

Warren shook his head. "Not yet. She was so tired she went straight to bed. Ricardo's staff found her some shampoo, toothpaste, and a few things to wear."

"Right now bed sounds good to me too." Jeff sighed. He hauled himself out of the chair and shuffled down the hall.

Jeff woke early Friday morning to the sounds of children playing outside his window. Peering out, he scanned the streets. Above the rich colors of the city, he saw the shoulders of the Andes mountains. The horizon was half-hidden in a rainy mist.

Pulling on his blue jeans, shirt, and light sweater, Jeff tiptoed out of the room so he wouldn't wake K.J., who was still snoring lightly. Since the bristling sun was already breaking through, he knew he wouldn't need the sweater very long.

"Good morning," Jeff said cheerily when he found Ricardo.

"Breakfast is almost ready." Ricardo pulled hot muffins from the oven. "One of the cooks made these before he went to start breakfast at the center this morning."

Just then, Warren hurried in. "I told Mindy about the arrest."

"How'd that go?" Jeff asked.

"She'll be fine." Warren smiled.

"I don't understand how you got through Customs without your luggage being searched." Ricardo was stroking his moustache again. "El Dorado airport is famous for long lines and detailed searches. You would have noticed the wrong bag."

"I don't know how it happened either." Warren reached for a muffin. "The officials waved us straight through. We must have looked innocent."

"Yep. I'm innocent," K.J. said as he stumbled into the kitchen, rubbing his eyes. "Whatever Mindy says I did now, I swear it wasn't my fault. Couldn't be. I just woke up."

Mindy swatted him as she walked past, but she was grinning. It was the first time since their arrival that she'd smiled big enough to show off her braces.

"Any news on my luggage?" she asked.

"Not yet," Ricardo replied. "We'll take the suitcase to the police station this morning. They'll get your luggage back. It's best that we don't get involved."

"I hope those drug dealers don't have it," Mindy added. "My name is on it. And information about where we're staying."

Warren got up, carrying his dishes to the sink. "Don't worry. It'll work out. I'll meet you back here after I'm finished lecturing at the university. Should be sometime after lunch. Why don't you spend the morning plotting the video shoot? Ricardo will take us to the center later so we can meet some street kids."

After Warren left, K.J., Jeff, and Mindy noisily did the dishes while Ricardo attended to some paperwork. The phone rang, and Jeff heard Ricardo pick it up. He hoped it was good news.

"It's for you, Mindy," Ricardo called.

As she dried her hands, Jeff wondered why anyone would call Mindy. *Must be someone from the airline,* he thought.

Everyone gathered around as Mindy picked up the phone and listened. In a matter of seconds, her eyes filled with terror.

"Who is it? What's wrong?" they all asked at once.

Mindy covered the receiver with her hand. "I think it's the drug dealers!" she whispered hysterically. "They want the suitcase."

Ricardo grabbed the phone and began speaking in Spanish. Jeff tried to understand, but the words flew by too fast. The team waited in silent anticipation.

The dark honey color drained out of Ricardo's face. Finally, he hung up the phone.

"What'd they say?" K.J. demanded.

"They have Mindy's suitcase and want to trade it," Ricardo answered. "But they want us to keep it until tonight because they're being watched."

"Then let's tell the police!" Mindy cried.

Ricardo hesitated then said slowly, "They also threatened to damage one of our centers if we go to the police."

He sat down and looked into their eyes. "You see, the drug cartel is very powerful in Colombia. They control the police—at least some of the police.

Life means nothing to them. They'd kill us on sight. Money and drugs are like enormous magnets. Once people get pulled into drugs, nothing but the Lord can pull them away. After a while, these people have no conscience."

Everyone's eyes grew larger.

"That's why people carry guns," Ricardo continued. "This is a dangerous situation. Our city is well known for beauty and brutality mingled together. We say it's like an orchid with a drop of blood at its heart."

"Wow," K.J. said. "Okay Mindy, give it up. You wouldn't wear all that girlie stuff anyway. Let's just trade 'em suitcases and get on with our work."

"That's probably the safest thing to do," Ricardo agreed.

"I wonder why that suitcase is so important," Jeff said.

"Didn't you see the clothes?" Mindy asked. "They're not my style, but they're very expensive. I'd want them back too."

Ricardo shook his head. "I don't think it's clothes they want. There must be something important inside. But let's not worry about that."

"Why?" Mindy wanted to know.

"Because what we don't know won't hurt us," Ricardo replied.

"This is all your fault, K.J. I'd better get my suitcase back." Mindy glared at him. "If it's lost, you'll be safer with those drug dealers than you'll be with me."

"I believe you, I believe you." K.J. raised his hands in the air.

"Let's forget that for now," Ricardo said sternly. "Let's get on with your mission. I think you need to spend some time planning the video. Then I'll show you around Bogota."

"I need to get the equipment ready," K.J. muttered. "I hope this altitude doesn't affect it. I'm still having a hard time catching my breath."

Later that morning, Ricardo took Jeff, Mindy, and K.J. to Carrera 15, one of Bogota's busiest streets. Jeff saw the fancy boutiques, jewelry stores sparkling with Colombian emeralds, and galleries of pre-Colombian art. The deep, rich colors the Colombians wore seemed to match the ancient culture.

Workers busied themselves cleaning the fronts of their shops. An old Indian woman sat on the sidewalk. Hanging behind her was a beautiful array of leather bags, sandals, and jackets. Nearby was a pastry store. Jeff smelled espresso coffee in the air.

"This stuff sure looks good," Mindy said with her nose pressed against the window of a candy store. She focused on brown sugar squares, bon bons, and other delights. She couldn't stand not trying some, so she and K.J. ducked in to buy a few pieces.

Ricardo smiled. "People say Colombia has a massive sweet tooth."

Jeff laughed, but he was busy watching well-dressed people hurry by. Mindy had said Colombians are known for their fancy, fashionable clothing—especially when they went out at night.

K.J. and Mindy returned and offered the others samples as they walked. Turning the corner onto Calle 85, Jeff spotted several expensive cars parked under the tall trees in front of a gallery. Green and white taxis dropped people in front. Nearby was a cooking cart filled with skewered corn cobs and bits of pork and beef.

Suddenly, a dozen scruffy children appeared out of an alley. They swarmed around the windows of the taxis, begging for money.

Instantly, Jeff's heart felt heavy. This was the real reason he'd come. He'd spent months praying for these kids. Now they were in front of him. Tears welled up in his eyes as he watched them ask strangers for money.

In his preparation for the trip, Jeff read about the serious conditions these kids lived in. He couldn't believe that children as young as four or five lived in cardboard boxes, alleys, under bridges—wherever they found a dry spot. He also couldn't believe that some of these kids weren't even orphans. Many had been turned out by their parents because they could make a better living on the streets.

Jeff felt guilty when he thought of his home. These kids had no lap to cuddle in, no one to read them stories, no one to fix their dinner. Unless they stole or begged, they didn't eat at all.

Jeff had prayed harder for these kids than he'd ever prayed for anything in his life. And as much as he hurt for these kids, he knew God's heart hurt even more.

A tiny, ragged-looking kid with a torn jacket ran

toward Jeff and Ricardo. He held up a battered yellow box of Chiclets gum.

"Señor! Señor! Chiclets, señor?"

The rest of the kids watched, staring up at them with sad, dirty faces. They looked more like starving dogs than children. Jeff felt his insides twisting with pain.

Before today, he'd never seen kids who looked old. But these kids did. They were barefoot, their skin mottled gray with filth. Except for one, they all looked under ten years old. The oldest boy had a scabbed swelling on the left side of his head. His eyes caught Jeff's.

· Jeff looked away for a moment. Then he noticed some of the kids surrounding K.J. and Mindy.

"What should we do?" Mindy asked in a panic.

"Let's give them some change," K.J. said in his easy, straightforward way. He dug into his jeans pocket.

The older boy ran over. "That's a good idea, señor. A good idea."

Jeff was shocked when he heard the boy speak nearly perfect English. "You speak English!" He smiled. "What's your name?"

"If I tell you, will you give me money?" the boy asked.

Jeff glanced at Ricardo, who was standing back, silently observing everything.

Jeff pulled some pesos out of his pocket. He placed them in the dirty, outstretched hand. "This is for you." He tried to look the boy in the eyes rather than stare at his head wound. "You don't have to tell me your name if you don't want to."

The boy hesitated for a moment. "My name is Antonio."

K.J., Mindy, and Ricardo gave each of the kids a couple of coins.

Jeff's heart melted. He wanted to give these kids all he had, to take them home with him, to do anything he could to help. But the problem seemed so overwhelming.

"Wow," was all Jeff could say as the kids ran back into the alley.

Ricardo lead them through a park entrance. "Let's relax here for a while," he suggested.

"How many street kids are in this city?" Jeff asked when they had found a bench to sit on.

"No one knows for sure, but they number in the thousands. I'm told there are 40 million in Latin America." Ricardo wiped his eyes. "The Spanish word is *gamines.* They're all over Bogota—packs of homeless kids living in alleyways and side streets. They live and die in the gutters and garbage-choked courtyards behind restaurants, begging, thieving, and selling whatever they can lay their hands on just to stay alive.

"The kids stay high most of the time," Ricardo continued, "by sniffing rubber glue used to make shoes. It's their way of numbing the pain. They'll kill each other for it."

Mindy eyes were filled with astonishment. "I noticed one boy was wearing a man's suit coat. How do they get their clothes?"

"They find whatever they can," Ricardo replied. "Their shoes are horrible—if they're lucky enough to have shoes."

"I don't care much about my suitcase anymore," Mindy said quietly. "I'd be embarrassed if these kids saw how much stuff I brought."

"Good thing I got rid of it for ya, huh?" K.J. laughed.

"You're not off the hook on that one yet." Mindy glared. "So cool it."

"Enough, you guys!" Jeff ordered. Their bickering bothered him. It seemed so trivial in light of what they had just witnessed. "They die in empty lots and courtyards?" he asked Ricardo.

"Yes. Scores of kids under five years old die every day in Bogota alone. Mostly of malnutrition."

"What do you mean, in Bogota alone?" Mindy asked.

"Every day, forty thousand kids die in the world," Ricardo answered. "Street kids live in every city in Latin America."

"We have street kids in the States," K.J. said intently. "But they're usually teenagers who've run away—not little kids who have been kicked out."

Ricardo's eyes teared up. "There are 100 million street kids worldwide who have to go out and make a living as a child. Millions support themselves by prostitution or drug trafficking."

"That's unbelievable!" Mindy exclaimed. "I thought the statistics I'd read were exaggerated. Kids in America don't understand. We don't realize how lucky we are."

Ricardo reached for his handkerchief. "That's why I've given my life for them. I'll do anything to serve people like you who come to help us."

"Do you think we can make a difference?" Jeff asked.

"Yes. You'll only be here for a short time, but you'll help us immensely if you get the word out. Mostly, we need long-term volunteers. It takes months to build relationships with these kids."

Ricardo took a deep breath and continued. "Sometimes we think we're making progress with them, but then one takes off and goes back to the streets. It's painful to watch. They've been so wounded that it's hard for them to trust anyone."

"Hopefully, our video will help," K.J. put in.

"It will," Ricardo said excitedly. "Besides workers, we need donations. It's expensive to run these homes. We're always short of money. There is so much more we could do if we only had more staff and more money."

Jeff smiled sadly. "Please pray we do the best we can. My dad is working on getting the video played across the nation. We hope it will raise money to help you start other homes."

Everyone sat quietly, trying to process what they had just experienced.

"What time is it, anyway?" Mindy asked after a few minutes.

"Eleven-thirty," Jeff replied.

K.J.'s mouth flew open, and he let out a scream. He stared at his empty wrist. "Where's my watch?"

Ricardo looked over at a stunned K.J. "Looks like you got robbed," was all he said. "Sorry. Bogota is known as 'Pickpockets City.' See if anything else is missing."

"That Antonio brat bumped into me," K.J. groaned. "I'll bet that's how he did it! And that's probably how he got that bump on his head—someone knocked him on his head when he tried it with them!"

"Is everyone else okay?" Ricardo asked.

"I'm fine," Mindy said, glancing at K.J. "Except for my suitcase."

Ricardo ignored her and looked around. "It would probably be wise to not wear any jewelry when you're out, especially at night. Crime is so bad here that our police sometimes train officers from New York and Los Angeles on how to spot and stop pickpockets."

Suddenly, Ricardo's eyes darted back and forth. His face showed alarm.

Jeff looked around to see what it was. "What's wrong, Ricardo?"

"Don't panic," Ricardo replied quietly. "But I think we're being followed."

Chapter 3

The Burgundy Suitcase

"What do you mean?" Jeff exclaimed.

"I think the cartel is dead serious about us staying away from the police," Ricardo replied. "I've seen the same two men in several places today. They're watching our every move."

"Where are they?" Mindy whispered.

"Don't look," Ricardo cautioned. "They're hidden behind those trees."

"Shouldn't we go to the police?" K.J. asked.

"They'd shoot us before we got in the door,"

Ricardo said matter-of-factly.

"What'll we do?" Mindy cried.

"Nothing." Ricardo stroked his moustache. "Let them watch us. We're not doing anything."

"Why doesn't somebody deal with them?" Jeff wanted to know.

"They're powerful people," Ricardo replied. "Sad to say, but Bogota's place in the world's headlines is always centered around drugs. Colombia may be famous for its delicious coffee and beautiful emeralds, but the cocaine trade is the biggest business. It is estimated that 60 percent of Colombians are somehow involved in the cocaine industry."

"Don't they realize what drugs do to people?" Jeff asked in exasperation. "What they do to families?"

"Colombians don't see it as a shameful occupation. They see it as a business," Ricardo explained.

"Do the Colombians grow the stuff?" K.J. tried to keep his voice calm.

"No. Most is grown in Peru and Bolivia. We have a saying in Latin America, 'The Colombians have all the brains, but the Bolivians and Peruvians have the coco plants.'"

"So Colombians sell cocaine from the plants their neighbors have grown?" Mindy asked.

"That's right." Ricardo nodded his head. "The Colombians are very smart. They have made cocaine a worldwide billion dollar business. And because the drug cartel controls most of the government officials, there is little to stop them. They've been known to murder opponents—including the police."

"I want to go home," Mindy cried. "They can keep my suitcase if they want."

K.J. shuddered. "Is Bogota the headquarters for drugs in Colombia?"

"It's powerful," Ricardo said, "but many of the big drug lords are in Medillin. Others come from Cali."

Jeff peeked out of the corner of his eye and saw the two men in expensive business suits. They were watching their every move.

Mindy broke his concentration. "Why doesn't the church do something?"

"Even though most Colombians belong to the Catholic Church, they're too frightened to get involved," Ricardo said sadly.

"No wonder there are thousands of kids here with problems!" Jeff felt annoyed.

"That's right," Ricardo agreed. "The drug cartel's presence creates a spirit of evil that dominates every part of the city."

"Why don't we pray against that spirit?" Jeff suggested. "We know it comes from Satan himself."

Everyone agreed.

Lifting his eyes toward the mountains, Jeff prayed. "Lord, You created the majestic beauty that surrounds Bogota. It's not Your plan that evil controls this city. We stand against the powers of darkness that rule here. Give us favor with the *gamines* and make our mission a blessing to the people of Bogota."

"Father," Mindy added, "forgive me for being so selfish. I have so much. Help me share with others."

"Forgive me too," K.J. pleaded, "for my anger

about my watch. It's only a thing. Help me regard people higher than things."

Everyone said Amen. Jeff felt a powerful peace.

Ricardo wiped his eyes and smiled. "Your prayers must have worked. Those men are gone."

"That's good," Mindy sighed. "Real good."

Ricardo laughed and then yawned. "It's time for a siesta. Then we'll get Warren and work on the video."

"Do you really take siestas here?" K.J. asked. "I thought that was a Mexican tradition."

Ricardo laughed. "Siestas are a tradition all over Latin America. Our workday is from eight to noon. Then everyone has lunch and takes a nap between twelve and two, and then we go back to work."

"That's sounds good to me," Jeff said. "I'm still tired from the trip. The altitude hasn't helped either."

"That's pretty normal." Ricardo smiled. "A nap will help. Let's go."

After an hour nap, Jeff woke at 2:15. The cool air and jet lag had made it easy to sleep.

K.J. hadn't slept at all. He was working on his Super 8 Canon camcorder. He was the Reel Kids' cameraman—and he was good at it. His love for cameras was like Mindy's love for computers.

Jeff preferred being in front of the camera, just like his anchorman dad and his mom, who worked as a part-time news correspondent for a network. He had decided to make it his career as well.

"So what's the plan this afternoon?" K.J. asked when he noticed Jeff was awake. "You ready for some action? Or did you plan to sleep all day?"

"Ricardo is taking us to Mount Monserrate," Jeff said. "We'll get to go on a Swiss-made cable car to the top of the mountain. There's an old church on the summit."

"Sounds like my kind of ride." K.J. grinned. "I just hope those guys don't follow us."

"I'm not going to live in fear. We're here on a mission. I once heard a missionary say, 'The safest place in the world to be is in the will of God.'"

"What does that mean?"

"That some people are killed by buses right in front of their own houses. But if you know God has sent you somewhere in the world, even if it's a dangerous place, He'll take care of you."

"I like that!" K.J. smiled as he grabbed his camera bag. "Then we don't have to worry about those thugs in the suits, do we? Let's go!"

Jeff and K.J. raced to the living room and found Warren and Ricardo discussing the suitcase.

"Have we heard from the cartel yet?" Jeff asked.

"No," Ricardo said. "They said they would call tonight before they came."

Jeff nodded. "How'd the teaching go at the university?" he asked Warren.

"Really well," Warren answered. "They want me to come back every morning for a week. But we'll see how things go here."

Ricardo nodded his head in agreement. "Are you guys ready? Better go find Mindy. It's almost three. This is a perfect time to visit Monserrate."

K.J. looked like he was about to boil over with excitement as they boarded the cable car. Mindy looked a little nervous, so Jeff stayed close.

In the distance stood the shrine of Monserrate. The sheer cliff looked like a drop curtain behind the city. An illuminated statue of the Virgin Mary stretched out her arms.

"I researched this," Mindy said. "The ride up is pretty steep. But the view from the top is supposed to be breathtaking."

"I don't know if I can go then," K.J. joked, leaning against the glass wall of the cable car and pretending to gasp for air.   "I've been out of breath since we got here."

Mindy ignored him and pointed toward the mountain. "There are restaurants up there. And cobblestone streets."

"I can't wait to see the view," K.J. said. "It'll be great footage!"

Ricardo grinned. "From the top, all of Bogota lies at your feet. In the center of the city, you'll see the skyscrapers thrusting up. Surrounding them are the buildings with their white walls and tiled roofs. And on the outskirts, the barrios."

As the cable car climbed, Jeff glanced at the other passengers. Most of them had cameras around their necks. Some looked like tourists from around the world, while others were Indians and native Colombians. His eyes stopped on a tall, dark man in a double-breasted business suit. The man stared at Jeff. His squinty eyes looked deadly.

Jeff turned to see if Ricardo had noticed. Sure enough. As soon as he made eye contact with Ricardo, Jeff knew he was aware of the man too.

K.J. aimed his camera, scanning smiling passengers, the cable car, and the cliffs along the way. The footage would be an excellent backdrop for the street kids' story.

As Jeff watched his buddy, he realized K.J. had picked up on much of what was going on. He saw the camera stop momentarily on the face of the man in the double-breasted suit.

Very smart, Jeff thought. They might need the picture for some sort of identification later.

Traveling higher, Jeff tried to forget the stranger. He did a quick interview with Ricardo for the video. The other passengers looked on, amused.

Finally, they reached the top and the door opened. Jeff jumped off, followed by the others. He stepped out into a ripping wind. Trees had few leaves at this altitude. The view of the mountains was overwhelming. Jeff stood amazed at the sight of Bogota far below them. Red-tiled roofs were everywhere, dwindling into the distance.

"Hey, Jeff," K.J. shouted, pointing to Bogota. "Remember playing with our Matchbox cars when we were little? Our cities were about that size."

"About the same size all right, but this is much more beautiful!"

Single file, they trudged towards the large church.

"On Sundays," Ricardo called over his shoulder, "thousands from Bogota swarm up this mountain to 'keep a promise' to the statue of the Fallen Christ."

"Why don't they talk to the living Christ?" Mindy asked.

"It's something they've done for years," Ricardo replied.

"As a tribute to Mary, some even carry crosses. Others climb the hill on their knees."

Jeff approached the beautiful chapel and then saw two restaurants. K.J. filmed everything in sight while the others looked around.

From the city, the church had looked stark and white. But from up here, it was a mellow yellow color, with crumbling bricks and wooden doors that had turned a weathered blue. Beggars, faces brown and leathery from the sun and wind, sat on the steps of the church.

"Reading about this place was incredible," Mindy said. "But I never thought I'd see all this. The church was built in the seventeenth century."

Jeff nodded. Suddenly, he spotted the man in the double-breasted suit. He was walking straight toward him and, to his surprise, he kept coming closer.

Jeff looked for the others, but they had disappeared around a corner. His heart flip-flopped as the man stopped right in front of him and looked him in the eye.

"Señor," the man said, "my name is Carlos Lopez. My job is to keep an eye on you. If you don't do as we say, your sister could have a serious accident. Maybe on the ride down."

Jeff gasped, unable to catch his breath. Then the man turned away, hurried to the cable car, and got on.

Jeff's heart pounded with fear. He hadn't moved from the spot, but he was trembling inside. He shook his head, trying to snap out of it. Then Ricardo and Warren walked up.

"You look like you saw a ghost," Warren joked.

"Worse than that," Jeff finally found his voice. "The guy in the suit confronted me. His name is Carlos. He threatened to hurt Mindy."

"What'd you tell him?" Ricardo asked.

"Nothing. I was too frightened to speak. He left on that cable car." Jeff pointed to the cable car in the distance.

Warren put his arm around Jeff. "It's okay, Jeff. He was just trying to scare you. Mindy's with K.J. right around the corner. Let's go get them, finish filming, and go back. We'll get something to eat along the way."

Jeff was glad to be off the cable car. He felt better with his feet on solid ground again. He'd stood so close to Mindy that she'd complained he was smothering her all the way down.

After dinner, Ricardo and Warren sat in the kitchen, waiting for the dreaded phone call. K.J. was reviewing his video shots, and Mindy began writing the script to go with them.

Sitting alone in the living room, Jeff tried to deal with the fears that made him tremble. In his mind, he knew he and his friends were safe. But there was a piece of his heart that was still afraid.

Scriptures filled his mind. He quoted some of

his favorite verses in Psalm 91 to himself. "A thousand shall fall at your side, and ten thousand at your right hand, but it will not happen to you."

The words fed his soul, and he got stronger by the minute. He had come on a mission, and he would not be defeated. In a few moments of prayer, he committed Mindy and the others to God for His protection.

Then he remembered what Ricardo said about the street kids. He feared the video wouldn't be enough. He wanted to do more.

His thoughts turned to Antonio, the young gang leader they had met. He could be a great leader if only God would turn his life around.

K.J. suddenly bounded into the room, startling Jeff from his thoughts.

"Jeff, you won't believe what Mindy and I found!"

"What is it?" He noticed a hint of fear in K.J.'s voice.

"Follow me," K.J. called as he ran from the room.

Jeff raced behind K.J. into Mindy's room. The suitcase lay opened on the bed. Mindy was trembling.

"Look at this!" K.J. exclaimed.

Jeff watched as K.J. pulled some clothes away and lifted up the ruffled lining under them. Jeff could see what looked like a tiny hole in the bottom of the case. He was stunned.

"It looks like a secret compartment!"

Chapter 4

Serious Threats

K.J. carefully removed clothes and cosmetics to get a better look.

"Should we be doing this?" Mindy whispered over his shoulder. "They're going to know we searched it."

"We'll put it back the way it was, Mindy," K.J. said. "Didn't you notice me shooting some footage of this case? I know exactly how things were packed. But if we can find some evidence in here, we can nail these guys."

"They'll nail us first," Mindy sighed. "In a coffin."

Jeff smiled nervously at her. "We'll be careful, Mindy. Very careful."

"Shouldn't we get Warren and Ricardo?" Mindy asked.

"Let's have a look first," Jeff insisted. "The fewer people who know about this, the better."

K.J. began to pull clothes out. First was a pale pink wool suit with a sequined design on one shoulder.

"Wow, Mindy. Wouldn't Mom like that one?"

"Yeah." Minded nodded with a smile. "She has a sweater dress with sequins like that. This lady has great taste."

K.J. held up three silk blouses in varying shades of pink. Everything was perfectly folded. Then he pulled out a pink belt and pink stockings, all tucked neatly into pairs of pink shoes.

"This gal sure likes pink," K.J. laughed, reaching the bottom of one side of the suitcase.

"Looks normal to me," Mindy said.

When K.J. tapped on the bottom of the case, there was a dull echo. It sounded hollow.

Jeff turned to Mindy. "Could you get us a knife from the kitchen?"

"Okay," she said, rolling her eyes. "I guess I'm already an accomplice." She hurried out of the room.

Shortly, she brought back a sharp steak knife. "This is the best I could find."

"It's perfect," K.J. said with a laugh. "Perfect."

K.J. slid the knife carefully along the beautiful

lining. Now that they had gone this far, Jeff hoped they would find something.

"Jackpot!" K.J. cried.

Jeff and Mindy both held their breath. K.J. pried up with the knife. Jeff couldn't believe his eyes. The entire floor of the suitcase was lifting.

"I think I've got it." Sweat glistened on K.J.'s brow. He hesitated. "Ladies and gentlemen, drum roll, please."

A thin balsa-wood board popped up. K.J. eased the whole board out. It was covered with the same fabric as the original bottom of the Samsonite case.

Everyone stared. Several packages, carefully wrapped in paper, were wedged in the bottom of the suitcase.

"Close it back up," Mindy ordered. "I don't want to know what's in there."

"It's okay." Jeff reached for a packet. "We need to know what we're dealing with." He unwrapped it slowly.

"It's probably drugs," Mindy cried.

"You don't bring drugs *in* to Colombia," K.J. reminded her. "You take them *out*."

"Then what is it?" Mindy cried.

Everyone gasped in unison. Jeff gingerly held the unwrapped package and stared into his hands— a stack of new hundred dollar bills.

"There must be thousands of dollars here!" K.J. nearly shouted.

"This must be how they launder money," Jeff said.

"How?" Mindy stared in disbelief.

"I'm surprised you missed this in your research," Jeff kidded.

"Well, I didn't study drug smuggling!" Mindy answered defensively.

"This is how they get illegal money back into the country. If they hide it, they don't have to declare it when they go through Customs. Then they don't have to pay tax on it." Jeff held the money to the light.

"Now we've got to tell Ricardo and Warren!" Mindy's eyes almost popped out. "This could get us killed."

"You're right," Jeff agreed. "Ricardo will know what to do."

"I sure hope so," Mindy sighed.

Jeff's heart raced wildly as he ran to the dining area where Warren and Ricardo were having a cup of coffee. When he reached them, the panicked look on his face froze their coffee cups in mid-air. He quickly told them what they had done and what they had found.

"Okay." Warren's face was pale. "Let's have a look."

They hurried to the bedroom. Ricardo studied the contents of the case. Then Warren unwrapped the other packets, and Ricardo started counting the money.

Everyone hovered in silence until he finished. Ricardo looked like someone had shocked him. "There's over fifty thousand dollars here."

"What do we do?" Jeff asked.

"I don't know," Ricardo said. "We're really in a mess now."

"I told them not to open it," Mindy cried.

"It doesn't matter," Ricardo hushed her. "Just

having this case got you in trouble. Now we need to figure out how to get out."

"See, K.J.," Mindy snapped. "You've done it again."

"I thought you finally forgave me for the mixup." K.J. hung his head.

"I did forgive that, but digging up this money? I don't know."

"Okay. Okay." Warren held his hand up. "This won't solve anything."

"Maybe we'll *have* to go to the police," Mindy said.

"That probably won't help." Ricardo stroked his moustache. "I think we should just put everything back and get rid of the case. Then hope for the best."

"What will they do to us if they know we saw the money?"

Mindy asked.

"I used to work in an upholstery shop," Ricardo said. "I think I can put it back together so they won't even know. Good thing you got it on video before you took it apart, K.J. That was a brilliant idea."

The phone rang and everyone jumped. They followed Ricardo to the phone and watched him ease it off the hook. Jeff held his breath. What if the drug dealers wanted the suitcase before Ricardo had a chance to put it back together?

Ricardo motioned for Mindy. "They want to talk to you," he whispered. "I'll pick up the other line."

Mindy took a deep breath and reached for the phone. "Hello," she said weakly.

After a few minutes, she slowly hung up the phone. Her face was as white as the plaster walls.

"What's wrong, Mindy?" Jeff, K.J., and Warren asked in unison.

Before she could answer, Ricardo came running back. "They want to wait another day to pick it up."

"That's great news!" Jeff exclaimed. "Min, why are you so frightened?"

Mindy burst into tears, and Ricardo reached out and hugged her. She looked at Jeff with terror in her eyes.

"They threatened to hurt Mom and Dad."

Chapter 5

Love in Action

Everyone sat down, numbed by what they heard.

"How do they know where we live?" Jeff asked, his voice low.

Ricardo held Mindy's hand. "They could be bluffing. But your address was on your suitcase, wasn't it?"

Mindy wiped her eyes. "Yes. Our address was on my name tag."

"We'll call your parents tonight," Warren said.

Mindy checked her watch. "They won't be home until late. There's a church banquet tonight."

"I don't think they'll mind us calling late for this." Warren smiled.

"You're right," Mindy sighed. "Meanwhile, I'd like to pray for them."

Everyone bowed their heads.

"Oh, Father," Mindy began, her voice shaking, "it scares me to think my parents are in danger. Please send angels to guard them. In Jesus' name, we claim Your protection. Amen."

The others echoed Amen in agreement.

"I'm really tired," Mindy said quietly. "I want to go to bed."

Jeff leaned over and gave her a hug.

"You've all had a full day," Warren said. "Let's get to bed. Our minds will be clear in the morning."

"Let me get the suitcase," Ricardo said. "I'll work on it tonight."

The sunlight hotly blazed into Jeff's room early Saturday morning. Gathering his thoughts, he wished everything had been a bad dream, but he knew better.

K.J. was absolutely still, except for light snoring. Jeff looked at his watch. It was 6:30 a.m.

Knowing he needed wisdom, Jeff reached for his Bible. As he opened it, he immediately saw 1 Corinthians 13—the chapter about love. He sensed God wanted to speak to him. As he read, he knew God was showing him the way out of all this—through love.

Jeff felt new strength. He knew love would work with the kids, but he wondered how love could solve the suitcase mess.

Ricardo was in the kitchen when Jeff got there after showering and dressing. He looked tired.

"How was your sleep?" Ricardo asked.

"Good. Have you seen Warren yet?"

"He's already gone to a breakfast meeting with one of the professors. He talked with your parents last night, and everything was fine there. They all know you're in the right place."

Jeff chuckled. "I'm sure Mom has already called the church prayer committee. They're very faithful about praying for us on these trips."

"They said not to worry about them."

"Good. Did you finish the suitcase?"

"I'll let you guys have a look. I don't think the drug dealers will notice a thing."

"Do they always use suitcases to smuggle things?" Jeff asked.

"No. Suitcases are actually outdated. Nowadays, they use air compressors, furniture, stereo speakers, Nintendo tapes, dolls, hollowed-out televisions—almost anything you can think of."

Ricardo turned the heat down on the stove. "I once heard of a case where they cut a bowling ball in half and found $210,000 in hundred dollar bills."

Jeff laughed and shook his head. "Think I'll go see how Mindy is doing this morning," he said, excusing himself. "She'll be glad to hear Mom and Dad are okay."

When Jeff and Mindy got back to the kitchen, K.J. and Ricardo were eating breakfast and laughing at other crazy ways people had been caught smuggling.

"So what kind of adventure do you have for us today, Ricardo?" Mindy asked as she sat down.

"I think you guys *brought* the adventure." Ricardo smiled. "Today, we're going to work at one of our centers."

"Great! Can I do some filming?" K.J. asked.

"We'll have to ask Flora, the young woman who runs the center, and let the *gamines* know what's happening. She and a few other staff live upstairs. They sometimes take in kids who want to make a change in their lives. But the main ministry is feeding street kids and handing out clothing.

"And K.J.," Ricardo looked him in the eye, "please keep a close eye on your camera."

"You can say that again!" K.J. laughed, holding up his watchless arm.

"Has the government had any success with the street kids?" Jeff asked.

Ricardo shook his head. "Their efforts haven't been successful. The greatest opposition comes from the police. They even take *gamines* outside the city and beat them. Some have been killed. The government doesn't know what to do with them."

"What do you mean?" Mindy asked. "Why don't they just take care of them?"

"Before long, many people who offer them food and clothes feel like they've been used. You see, the *gamines'* trust with the adult world has been broken. They are deeply wounded, so kindness sometimes threatens them more than being treated badly."

Mindy looked confused. "You're telling me they would rather be treated badly?"

"It's the language they understand," Ricardo replied sadly. "They deal with their pain by ripping people off and taking advantage of their kindness. It's their way of controlling their own lives. They hurt you before you can hurt them."

"Then why do anything at all?" Mindy asked.

"That's exactly the approach the government workers have taken. They feel like fools for trying to help. They get cold and cynical after a while—which proves to the *gamines* that nobody is trustworthy. So the government doesn't do much at all anymore."

Jeff thought back to the Scriptures he'd read. Love was the key.

"Today, I think you'll see why we have some success," Ricardo said. "We build long-term relationships. Then we wait for the right moment for God to turn the key to their hearts."

Jeff couldn't hold back anymore. "In my devotions this morning, the Lord revealed the key. It's God's love. Jesus gave and gave—even when He was rejected."

"And don't be surprised if you're rejected when you try to help," Ricardo said, getting up from the table. "Let's just clean up a bit. Then we'll go to the center."

Although the center was only a few blocks from the ICC house, Jeff knew he was in a different part of town. The street was busy with traffic and crowded with beggars, cripples, and a lot of teenagers.

As they rounded a corner, Jeff saw two haggard-looking kids facing each other, crouched and tense. Both had their left arms wrapped in jackets. Knife blades flashed in their right hands. They used their jacketed arm as a sort of shield.

Jeff felt a sense of panic and looked to Ricardo and the others. Wasn't anybody going to stop them?

The small boys circled each other slowly, looking for an opening. One wore a filthy baseball cap with a leaping orange tiger on the back. The words *NO FEAR* were printed on it.

Jeff stood frustrated, waiting for someone to stop the fight. Ricardo appealed to the boys to put down the knives, but they both sneered back at him and continued circling.

A frightened crowd formed. Even the adults stood back, watching.

Suddenly, one boy jumped at the other. The one in the tiger cap cried out in pain as the knife slashed his right arm.

He fell to the ground. Blood gushed from the wound. The other boy stood still while his victim tried to stagger up. He was yelling and cursing, wild to go on.

Without thinking, Jeff rushed in to help. The wounded boy instinctively whirled his knife toward Jeff. Ricardo ran over and grabbed the knife. He pleaded with the boy in Spanish.

Jeff understood some Spanish, but Ricardo spoke so fast that Jeff had no idea what he said. Whatever it was, it worked. The attacker ran off, and his gang followed.

Clutching his arm, the wounded boy slowly got up. Ricardo helped him hobble down the street.

When they had gone a block or so, Jeff saw a crowd of street kids playing in front of a doorway. He knew it must be the center.

The building was older and bigger than the ICC house. The white paint was faded, and the windows were cracked. Patches on the red tile roof were obvious. But as they entered, Jeff sensed something that set this building apart from the rest of the block. He felt welcome.

Ricardo motioned for them to sit at long tables in the large, open room. He disappeared down a hall with the bleeding boy. From the kitchen sink, several people looked up to smile and wave.

Hungry-looking kids eyed them warily then went back to devouring the food on their plates. Others rummaged through boxes of clothes and shoes.

Jeff was still trembling from the ordeal on the street. Mindy and K.J. were jumpy too. They sat down, watching, but no one spoke.

Then a young woman with black, flowing hair appeared from the direction Ricardo had gone. Jeff's mouth fell open. *She's beautiful,* he thought. He studied every graceful step as she approached.

K.J., who had been watching the children, jumped to his feet when he saw her. Her dark eyes flashed when she smiled shyly.

"Welcome to our center," she said with a rich Spanish accent. "My name is Flora. I work with our precious *gamines*. Ricardo asked me to show you around."

Jeff's face flushed a little. Nervously, he shook

Flora's hand. Jeff guessed her to be in her twenties. *Not much older than I am,* he thought.

She wore a simple white blouse. Around the hem of her black skirt, dozens of embroidered children danced in bright shades of red, green, and yellow.

"It's nice, really nice, to meet you, Flora," Jeff stumbled over his words. "How can we help today?"

"Let me show you around," she replied as she shook Mindy's hand. "Then we'll get you started serving meals." She grinned at K.J., who blushed. Her smile was dazzling.

"This room is where we spend most of our time," she began as she walked. "The *gamines* come and go during the day. They eat at these tables. In that corner are some game tables."

Pointing at a jumble of ragged boxes in the corner, she said, "You've seen our clothing distribution system. Our office is where Ricardo went to bandage that boy. Upstairs are our living quarters. A visitor once told me the rooms reminded him of an old army barracks, but we're comfortable here."

Jeff and K.J. elbowed each other in an effort to get closer to Flora, but she continued without appearing to notice the scuffle.

"Three bedrooms are occupied by staff. We keep the others open for kids who want to get off the streets. We help them with schooling or job training. The younger ones are usually transferred to one of our rural centers where there is more of a family atmosphere."

"All this is provided for free?" Jeff asked.

"Well, not exactly," Flora continued. "While they are here, they must attend church and Bible studies. They also help with cleaning and meal preparation."

"What a wonderful ministry." Jeff rubbed his hands together. "How can we help?"

"I hear you're going to make a video about the centers. That should help a lot."

"No, no, I meant today. We're ready to go to work."

"Come on." Flora motioned with her hands. "I'll introduce you to the kitchen."

As they followed Flora, Ricardo came out of the office.

"Is the boy okay?" Jeff asked.

"He'll be fine. Our nurse is bandaging his arm. I have to go pick up Warren. I want to introduce him to a couple other people and show him the other centers. You'll be okay here with Flora?"

"Oh, yes. I'm sure we'll be fine," Jeff replied. A smile filled his insides, but he didn't let it show on his face.

"Flora knows what to do," Ricardo said. "Just don't wander away from here."

When Ricardo left, the team got busy. Jeff laughed and got out of the way when Flora handed Mindy a huge knife to chop apples, celery, and carrots. K.J. carried buckets of vegetables in cold water back and forth from the cooler.

A moment later, Jeff saw street kids laughing and pointing toward the kitchen. He just shook his head. K.J. was waltzing with the mop as he cleaned up the mess he'd made.

Flora put Jeff to work wiping up tables and helping little children fill their plates. He remembered the Scripture in 1 Corinthians 13. Love was the key. His heart filled with compassion thinking about it.

To his surprise, the kids didn't seem afraid of him. He was determined to love them no matter what happened. Four- and five-year-olds were easy to love—even if they rarely smiled. But God filled his heart with compassion for the older ones as well. Jeff felt like a big brother in a huge family.

After an hour or so, Flora walked up. "Would you like a break?" she asked.

"I'm doing fine. How about you?"

Flora smiled. "Well, I have been busy since five o'clock this morning. But God gives me His strength."

Jeff looked at her. "How long have you worked here?"

"Two years now. Before that, I couldn't stand seeing kids with guns, knives, and terrible lives on the streets. After all, they are just kids. I had been a Christian for years, but I wasn't doing anything about this. Their faces haunted me. I finally had to do something."

"The world needs more people like you, Flora."

"That's nice of you to say," Flora replied with bright eyes. "We do what we can. If we can get them clothes, food, showers, and sometimes housing, it's worth it. Sometimes, we put on puppet shows and have special meetings."

Flora paused. "Ricardo mentioned that you would be willing to speak to the kids. We have a devotion right after the main lunch. I'd be glad to interpret for you."

Jeff felt butterflies flutter in his stomach. He scanned the crowd of ragged, tough-looking kids. "Sure," he said, swallowing hard. "I've never spoken to street kids before. But I trust that God will give me something to say."

Suddenly, the room quieted as a gang of kids filed in. Jeff recognized them as the group they'd given the coins to on the street earlier.

The leader, like a small stallion guarding his herd, was the last to enter. He circled around to check on them. When he turned, Jeff saw the scabbed wound on the side of his head. It was Antonio—the one K.J. thought had stolen his watch.

Chapter 6

Antonio

Antonio and his group shuffled around the room like they owned it.

Jeff glanced toward the kitchen where K.J. stood frozen in his tracks. Obviously, he had recognized Antonio and wanted his watch back.

K.J. put down a platter of sandwiches and started toward Antonio. Jeff knew all he could do was pray.

With his hands in his pockets, Antonio met Jeff and Flora at the serving table. K.J. moved in, then stopped a few steps behind them.

Antonio stood in front of Jeff. "We meet again, señor."

"Yes," Jeff replied. "I'm glad to see you, Antonio."

With a look of determination, K.J. stepped forward to face Antonio. "I need to talk with you," he said boldly.

Jeff saw the sneer on Antonio's face. Even though K.J. was bigger, Jeff knew Antonio was tougher. Flora's glance darted from one to the other as they stood face to face.

"My watch was missing after you and your friends left," K.J. went on. "I know you took it."

Jeff prayed silently. By her stillness, Jeff knew Flora was praying too.

K.J. stepped closer, reaching into his back pocket. Antonio's body tensed like he was ready to spring. His gang closed in around him.

K.J. pulled out his wallet, smiling kindly. "One of you took my watch," he said, drawing out several bills. "I don't know why, but I want to forgive you. You must have needed the money, so I want to help. Here's some American dollars for whatever you need."

Jeff's mouth opened in astonishment. Flora's eyes glistened with tears. Mindy wiped her cheeks. K.J.'s eyes just sparkled.

Antonio held back for a second, then he reached for the money. He returned a cold smile, and his gang laughed nervously.

Jeff broke the silence. "We'd like you guys to stay for lunch."

Flora nodded her approval. "We're having a special meeting today. These Americans want to speak to us for a few minutes after lunch."

Antonio laughed. "Okay, we'll stay. But it better be good. We've heard it all before."

Antonio and his ragged little gang sat down to soup and sandwiches. After lunch had been served to everyone, Jeff, K.J., Flora, and Mindy quickly excused themselves. Flora led the team to a private room for prayer.

"Why did you do that, K.J.?" Jeff kept patting his buddy on the back. "You blew me away. That was the perfect example of the 'love in action' our pastor always talks about."

"I started thinking about love being the key." K.J. smiled. "Everybody was mean and nasty to Jesus. He got ripped off, but He just kept giving. I thought I'd try it. That's what we're here for, isn't it?"

After a short time of prayer, Flora walked back into the dining room and faced the crowd. Standing on a small platform, she introduced the members of the club. Flora explained the reason for their visit and about the video they were filming. K.J. had his camcorder rolling, and Mindy was taking notes.

No one applauded when Jeff walked up after Flora's introduction. Instead, the room got quiet. Nervously, Jeff looked out over the crowd.

As he began, he scanned the back of the room. The boy wounded in the knife fight was still sitting alone. Jeff's heart filled with compassion. He saw through the dirt and the tough exteriors. He felt like the Lord was allowing him to see through their anger, all the way to the pain that caused it.

"Flora explained that we're a media club from America called the Reel Kids. We're making a video to raise money to help this center."

Jeff waited for Flora to translate. He was glad to have her there. While she put his words into Spanish, he had time to think about what he was going to say next.

"But the real reason we're here today is to talk about a friend of ours you might want to meet."

Jeff glanced across the room. The kids were listening, but he noticed several who looked like little lions ready to attack. "This friend didn't have a place to live. He was hurt by almost everyone He met. He didn't even have a place to lay His head. He should have built walls to protect Himself like everybody else. Instead, He kept giving."

Flora translated slowly.

"He loved kids, especially those who didn't have mothers or fathers. He told them about His Father. He came to introduce His Father to kids who didn't have one."

Flora blinked back tears. Mindy stared at her brother.

"He showed kids how special they were to Him. Many of them found the peace and love they had searched for by becoming part of His Father's family."

K.J. filmed everything. Mindy stopped taking notes and let the tears roll down her face.

Jeff felt words flow from his lips. He went on, explaining how he joined the Father's big family years ago. "Some of you have very deep hurts and wounds from people who have continually abused you. I can see the pain in your eyes. The way to get free from that pain is to forgive those who have hurt you. Jesus bled from abuse from His angry enemies. But He forgave them to show them the power of love."

Tears left shiny tracks down Flora's face. She moved her hands in front of her heart to express Jeff's words.

"Jesus asked His Father to forgive them. He loves everyone and wants us all to be in His family. You can be a child for the first time. God's child."

Jeff paused for a few seconds. Then he turned to K.J. "I want my friend K.J. to tell his story. His dad left when he was young."

Jeff traded places with K.J. and took over as cameraman. Jeff knew K.J. was more comfortable behind the camera than on stage, but he also felt that K.J. had something important to say. He encouraged his best friend with a nod.

K.J. stepped up, took a deep breath, and began. "I know what it's like to lose part of my childhood. My dad left my mom and me when I was very young. I thought it was my fault. I felt abandoned. I didn't think anyone cared about me. I still remember how much it hurt."

The kids were listening intently.

"I can't even imagine what some of you have gone through. But I have a new Father now. And I'm here to tell you how you can have Him too."

Some of the little ones sniffled. Jeff knew K.J. was touching hearts by being honest about his own hurts and fears.

K.J. took a step closer to the kids. "Look. We

have nothing to offer. But we know someone who can make your childhood dreams come alive. Jesus told everyone that His kingdom was like that of a child. He is looking for kids to embrace His love. Please come and talk to us if you are interested in joining God's family."

Two boys started to applaud as K.J. finished, but snickering from Antonio's gang quickly made them stop.

With tears wet on her cheeks, Flora prayed a closing blessing on the kids.

In a few moments, the place hummed with laughter. A couple of kids were posing for K.J.'s camera and helping him film. Others played table games. Some of them started a soccer game behind the center.

Flora approached Jeff and Mindy while they dried the lunch dishes. "That was really special, Jeff. Your message needs to be heard by all the kids. No religious talk, just reality."

"That's the message of our club," Jeff said, smiling. "Warren keeps telling us to be real kids. If we preach at others, we have nothing to say. People are sick of religious words. They want to see the Father's love in action."

"That's right." Flora nodded. "These kids have seen too much talk and not enough action."

Jeff went to wipe the tables. He noticed Antonio and his gang preparing to leave.

Antonio approached Jeff. "Can I see you outside?" he asked.

Jeff had heard the same line from a school bully when he was ten, but he nodded anyway. He hoped

Antonio didn't intend to punch him like the bully had.

As Jeff followed Antonio outside, he prayed that this was a key moment in Antonio's life. Maybe his words had gotten through.

With his hands still in his pockets, Antonio took a few steps away from the doorway. He looked Jeff straight in the eye. "That was a bunch of garbage you told everybody in there. I grew up hearing all that Jesus stuff, and it stinks."

Jeff's heart sank with disappointment. This was not what he wanted to hear.

Antonio began to spit angry words. "You Americans travel here and tell us how to live. You talk about pain and hurt. But you don't have any idea what you're talking about. Come live on the streets for a while. I'll show you pain. And bring your Jesus too."

Antonio jerked up his shirt. Scars crisscrossed on his chest and stomach. "This is pain, man! Pain you or your Jesus know nothing about."

Jeff stood speechless. Antonio's words pierced him like poison darts. He wondered if his talk, if this entire trip, had been a waste of time.

Antonio shoved Jeff on the arm and turned away. "You can take your religious talk and stick it in your ear!" He called over his shoulder as he stomped off. His waiting gang followed obediently.

Jeff stood there for a moment, stunned. Then he slid down against the wall. He felt weak and discouraged. Why had they even come to Bogota? This street kid problem was too big. How could he have expected to make any difference when the government couldn't even make a dent in the problem?

From the doorway, Flora saw Jeff sitting on the cement. She walked over and sat beside him. "What's wrong, Jeff?" she asked quietly. "You look sick."

"I am." Jeff was embarrassed to have her see him like this, but he explained what had happened.

Flora looked at Jeff with understanding eyes. "Antonio has a very painful past."

"How's that?"

"His dad was in the drug cartel," Flora said. "Both of his parents were violent people. They continually abused Antonio when he was small. Antonio never knew what it was to be a kid."

"No wonder he's so angry." Jeff's mind raced. "Is that why he ran away from home?"

Flora's eyes filled with tears. "He didn't run away. When he was five, his parents were gunned down in their own living room. Antonio watched the whole thing. He stayed there with them for nearly two days before anyone found him. He was hiding in a closet."

She cleared her throat before she continued. "After that, his uncle took him in. That's where he learned to speak English. They were very wealthy."

"So why is he on the streets now?"

"His uncle was just as abusive as his father. Antonio's anger only made it worse. They couldn't cope and finally dumped him."

"How old is he?"

"Twelve."

"How do you know his story?"

"He and his gang are new to the center. And they only come to eat. But his friend told me about his past. Antonio doesn't talk about it."

Jeff's heart hurt for Antonio and all the pain he had experienced. Suddenly, he felt guilty for being so selfish. Antonio had been hurt badly, yet all Jeff had seen was his own discouragement.

"Flora," he finally said, "will you excuse me a moment? I think I need to be alone with God." He walked off across the back lot and leaned against a rickety wooden fence.

"Oh, Lord," he began, "please forgive me for being so selfish. Instead of thinking about Antonio's pain, I was worried about myself. Give me another chance. Forgive me for my lack of compassion."

Jeff felt better as he slowly walked back to the center. Flora was talking to some kids near the door. She turned to face him.

"I'm not giving up on Antonio," he told her. "I'm going to pray every minute for God to do something."

As Flora and Jeff turned to go inside, Warren and Ricardo came back. They all walked inside to join Mindy and K.J.

"How are things going?" Ricardo asked.

Flora smiled. "Very well. This is a special team God sent us. They're doing just great."

"We've had a productive time too," Ricardo replied. "Warren has been very helpful. He's given me some good ideas."

"Any word on the suitcase?" Jeff asked.

Warren shook his head. "That's why we came back."

"What do you mean?" Jeff pressed.

"We got another phone call. They're coming for the suitcase at midnight."

Chapter 7

Thief

Jeff didn't know what to say.

"They said they'll return Mindy's suitcase in a cardboard box," Warren added. "They want theirs in a box too."

"Do you think they'll know we found the secret compartment?" Mindy's eyes were wide.

"I don't think so," Ricardo replied. "I checked it carefully against K.J.'s tape. It looks good." He sighed. "But if they do figure it out, it will be the end of our ministry."

"What do you mean?" Jeff frowned.

"These men could wipe us off the face of the earth." Roberto shook his head. "As long as they believe we will return the suitcase, everything should be okay. But if they discover we found the money, they'll probably kill us."

"Shouldn't we go to the mayor or something?" K.J. demanded.

"That would be dangerous," Roberto said. "Remember, they control a lot of people. Everyone lives in fear. Even judges are afraid of them. They don't hesitate to shoot anyone."

"God will protect us," Jeff said. "He was watching when K.J. picked up the wrong case. He'll work it out."

"I hope so." Ricardo smiled at him.

"I made another call to your folks," Warren put in. "They haven't noticed anything peculiar. Your mom has the whole church praying. And K.J., she talked to your mom too."

"Are you sure they're not worried?" Mindy asked.

"Nope. They trust God to take care of you."

A group of kids shyly came over to drag Mindy and K.J. back to their ping-pong game. Laughing, they excused themselves. Cheers rose from the group of children.

Warren pulled out a piece of paper. "Ricardo would like to take me to meet a couple more people. Will you guys be okay here?"

"Fine," Jeff said as he glanced at Flora.

"I'll make sure they get back," Flora volunteered.

"It looks like you're in good hands." Warren looked from Jeff to Flora. "We'll meet you at the house for dinner around seven. You'll be finished by then, Flora?"

Ricardo and Flora looked into each other's eyes as if they shared a secret.

"We don't do this often," Ricardo began, "but the staff has decided to bless you guys with a Colombian steak feast. Please receive it as an expression of our love and appreciation."

"That sounds great!" Jeff exclaimed. "I just hope it's not our last meal."

"You'll be okay." Ricardo laughed, waving goodbye.

Flora looked at Jeff. "Are you feeling better?"

Jeff smiled and nodded.

"You guys can work here till we finish serving dinner if you'd like," she said.

"We'd be glad to." Turning to see what needed to be done, Jeff noticed the boy who'd been in the knife fight. He sat alone at the table, cradling his bandaged arm.

Jeff caught Flora's eye and nodded his head toward the boy. As if she could read his mind, she went to talk to him. A few minutes later she called Jeff over.

As he joined them, Jeff saw Flora's love for the hurting children. All day, he had watched how hard she worked to help the kids. At first, he had just noticed her outward beauty, but now he saw the beauty in her heart.

"Sit down, Jeff," she said. "Roberto wants to talk to you. I'll translate."

Jeff pulled a folding chair beside Flora and sat down. He guessed Roberto was around 10 years old. His face was scarred, his clothes were ragged, his dark eyes looked weary. And he smelled.

You can't judge people by the way they look, Jeff reminded himself. Smiling, he extended his hand across the table. "Nice to meet you, Roberto."

Jeff was embarrassed when Roberto couldn't get his bandaged arm over the table to shake hands, but Roberto just shrugged. Jeff and Flora smiled.

"Roberto, Flora said you wanted to talk to me."

Jeff waited for her to translate. He didn't know what to say, so he decided to listen first.

"Yes." Roberto nervously tapped his fingers on the table top. He fixed his gaze on the floor, avoiding eye contact. "You tried to help me out there. I wanted to thank you."

Jeff eyes softened. "I didn't do a very good job, but you're welcome anyway."

Roberto continued to look down. "This is my first time here. I like it."

Jeff looked at Flora as she translated his words.

"I've never heard words like yours today." Roberto still didn't make eye contact. "You made my heart warm."

Jeff focused his full attention on Roberto. While Flora translated, he prayed that God would reach the young boy.

"I never knew my parents. My mom wasn't married when I was born." Roberto raised his head but still wouldn't look at Jeff. He transferred his gaze to the wall. "She abandoned me in an alley. I was raised by street people. I got sick of being beaten and finally left them. I know the pain you talked about."

Finally, Roberto looked at Jeff. "Please tell me more about this Father's love."

When Flora finished translating Roberto's words, Jeff couldn't believe his ears. He grabbed Roberto's hand. Roberto clasped it for a brief moment, then slipped it out of his reach, glancing around to see if other kids were watching.

Jeff didn't want to miss the moment. "Roberto, God can restore your childhood. You are so young, yet you have experienced terrible things God never planned for you."

Flora translated.

"He's got a beautiful plan for your life," Jeff continued. "Your pain breaks His heart. One of God's names is 'Abba,' which means 'Daddy.' He wants to be your Daddy, Roberto."

Jeff paused a moment before going on. "Jesus came so you could join the family of God. You're the most important person in the world to Him. It's no accident we walked by you today while you were fighting."

"What do I have to do?" Roberto asked.

Tears were rolling down Flora's cheeks, and she was having trouble speaking. Jeff handed her a Kleenex from a box on the next table.

"Just ask Jesus to take over your life," Jeff said simply. "Ask the Father to become your Daddy. He'll be the Father you never had. Jesus died so that we might live forever in our Dad's home."

"How can this happen?" Roberto pressed.

Jeff smiled. "All you have to do is pray."

"Pray. Right here?"

"We can go to a private room if it makes you more comfortable. The important thing is what you do, not where you do it."

Flora nodded.

"So how will a prayer change my life?" Roberto looked confused. "I'll be back on the street in a couple of hours. You'll go back to America after you finish your video. I'll still be here."

When Flora finished the translation, she spoke to him in Spanish. Jeff could only understand a few of her words, so he waited patiently. As he sat there, he saw Mindy and K.J. talking to some other kids while another staff member translated for them. His heart beat faster. The Reel Kids Club was in full action. God was at work.

Flora finished and turned to Jeff. "I asked him to stay with us here at the center. There's a vacant bunk upstairs. I told him he could stay as long as he liked."

"That's great, Flora! Could he come to dinner with us tonight?"

Flora grinned, her eyes sparkling. "I don't see why not."

"Can we pray with him?"

"He wants to."

"Let's go over there," Jeff said, pointing to the room where Roberto had had his arm bandaged. "It will be easier."

As Jeff and Flora led Roberto toward the office, Jeff noticed the other kids were watching closely.

Once in the room, Jeff simply explained the gospel. "A commitment to Jesus means a new beginning, a chance to live like your Father's son. And it means an end to the stealing and fighting you've done on the streets. Do you think you're ready to commit your life to Jesus?"

Roberto's eyes teared up. "I hate my life on the streets. I'll be glad to give it up. It was survival. I wish the other kids could be in this room too."

Jeff and Flora nodded in agreement.

"I think you're ready," Jeff added quietly.

Bowing their heads, Jeff led Roberto in a prayer. Flora translated, making it sound even more beautiful to Jeff.

"Jesus. I want to be Your son. Please be the Daddy I never had. Forgive all my sins. I let go of all the pain from my past, and forgive my parents for their mistakes."

Roberto repeated every word.

Jeff and Flora continued. "Please come into my life. Make me part of Your big family."

By the time they finished, Flora wept openly and Jeff fought to keep hot tears from rolling down his face. Roberto wiped his eyes with his bandaged arm.

When Roberto looked up, his shy smile went all the way to his eyes. Although he hadn't washed his face, it somehow appeared cleaner and younger than before. Jeff could see that there had been a radical change.

"Thank you," Roberto said. "Thanks for that prayer. I feel so different. So happy!"

Flora gave Roberto a hug, and then she hugged Jeff. Roberto hugged them back. Jeff wondered if these were the first hugs Roberto had ever had.

Everyone laughed and hugged and talked. When things quieted down, Jeff looked at his watch. It was almost five.

"Tonight the staff is treating our team to a steak feast," he said to Roberto. "We'd love to have you join us."

"Thank you," Roberto replied excitedly.

Flora got up. "Why don't you come with me, Roberto? I'll show you your new room."

Jeff walked back to the main room where Mindy and K.J. were playing games with the kids. He was glad everyone was having fun. These kids didn't laugh much on the streets.

In the half hour it took K.J., Jeff, and Mindy to clean up the center after dinner, Flora had gotten ready for the party. Shiny black curls cascaded around her face, and she wore a red blouse and a brightly printed skirt.

"She could win a Miss Universe contest," Jeff whispered to K.J. as she descended the stairs.

With his eyes as big as his camera lens, K.J. stepped up to Flora, bowed elegantly, and offered her his arm. Her smile was dazzling.

Mindy twirled her way into the room in a festive dress Flora had given her, reminding Jeff of Joseph in his coat of many colors.

When they arrived at Ricardo's, lively Spanish music was playing. Balloons and bright paper flowers decorated the dining room. The aroma of sizzling steak floated in from a backyard grill. Jeff's mouth watered. Tantalizing smells of spicy rice and beans filled the house.

But he couldn't get the faces of the street kids out of his head. He was uncomfortable eating so well, knowing most of them would go hungry tonight. Then he remembered the young boy beside him. At least Roberto was here. From head to toe, inside and out, he was a new person. His hair was combed. He was clean and dressed in clothes and shoes from the center. Only the bandage reminded Jeff of Roberto's old life. His smile and laughter were evident that his decision had been real. Jeff thought of this party as Roberto's welcome into God's kingdom.

Jeff and K.J. quickly went to their room to get cleaned up. Jeff couldn't find his new green shirt, so he settled for an old one. K.J. wore a striped shirt with red suspenders and a big black hat he had found in a local market.

The staff had thought of everything to make the evening special. *They deserve this treat,* Jeff thought as he looked around. *They sacrifice every day for the kids.*

The table setting was perfect. Colorful paper napkins on a white tablecloth made the simple dishes look festive. Jeff knew the staff didn't have much money, but they had certainly done a terrific job with what they had.

After dinner, the fun began. Their Colombian hosts did everything with gusto. Ricardo and the staff taught the team some Colombian dances.

Jeff and K.J. competed for the chance to dance with Flora. Mindy danced with everyone. Roberto was a little shy at first, but after a while he seemed to be having the time of his life. They laughed and talked until 11 o'clock.

Finally, everyone said goodnight. Ricardo drove the staff back to the center while K.J., Mindy, Warren, and Jeff sat in the living room, knowing that the midnight deadline was quickly approaching. Looking at his watch, Jeff hoped there would be an end to the problem with the drug cartel soon.

"How was your day?" Jeff asked, trying to keep the mood light.

"I can't believe how much I love those kids." Mindy plopped her feet on the coffee table. "K.J. and I are thinking of moving here someday. These kids need the love you talked about."

"Yeah," K.J. agreed. "Your talk made a difference. The kids said it made them think."

"You didn't do so bad yourself." Jeff smiled. "In fact, I think sharing your own experiences was even more effective than what I said."

Warren laughed. "If Jeff ever gets too long-winded, we know that he can be replaced!"

"What about you, Warren? How was your day?" K.J. asked.

"We made some visits today and set up some church meetings for tomorrow."

Ricardo came in, whistling. Warren turned to him. "Ricardo, I am so impressed with your work here. More people need to know about it."

"Thank you, Warren. We have very dedicated people here, that's for certain." Ricardo looked at the clock. "You'll have to excuse me. I need to check the suitcase one more time. I hid it in my closet."

Mindy, K.J., and Warren chattered on about the

things that had happened that day. Jeff sat and listened. He loved the excitement in the air.

Suddenly, Ricardo rushed back from the hallway. "Did any of you move the suitcase?"

Everyone shook their heads.

"Then it's been stolen."

Chapter 8

Earthquake

You're kidding!" Jeff cried.

"I wish I was. Some office equipment is also missing. I think we've been robbed." Concern crossed Ricardo's face.

"Robbed?"

"We've got to find it!"

"That Carlos guy will be here in 30 minutes!"

Ricardo hushed everyone. "Quiet. Quiet. Go search your rooms. Maybe it was moved somehow. We'll meet back here in 15 minutes."

Everyone hurried to their rooms. As the minutes ticked away, they all searched frantically—in closets, under bunk beds, behind dressers, inside, outside.

The rest of the staff helped turn the house upside down. Fifteen minutes passed like seconds. Jeff was the first to arrive in the living room. Mindy, K.J., and Warren were on his heels. The suitcase was nowhere to be found.

Ricardo walked into the living room, shaking his head. He looked tired. "A number of things are missing. Two staff members lost jewelry, clothes, and some money."

Suddenly, Jeff thought of something. "I'll bet that's what happened to the shirt I couldn't find."

"Nothing missing from my room," Mindy said. "But then, there was nothing much to take."

"I've lost a pair of jeans and a couple souvenirs I'd bought," K.J. added.

"Everything is fine in my room," Warren reported. "They must not have gotten to that part of the house."

"Has this happened before?" Jeff asked.

"Yes." Ricardo sighed. "We get robbed once in a while. But I think I know who did it."

Everyone leaned forward.

"My neighbor just told me he saw a group of small *gamines* running from the house earlier today." Ricardo hesitated. "The older kid was carrying a suitcase."

Jeff was afraid to ask the question. "Do you think it was Antonio?" he finally said.

"I think so." Ricardo nodded. "He fits the description perfectly."

"He must have followed us home yesterday to know where we live," K.J. muttered.

"Street kids are pretty smart," Ricardo said.

"We'll worry about the rest of the stuff tomorrow." Warren looked nervously at his watch. "Meanwhile, we've got the guy in the double-breasted suit to worry about."

"He'll be here in ten minutes," Ricardo said. "He's going to be very angry if we don't have the suitcase."

"We'll just have to be honest and tell him what happened and ask for more time." Jeff hoped he sounded more confident than he felt. "Then we'll have to find Antonio."

Ricardo laughed nervously. "I don't think he'll listen. And finding Antonio will be as hard as finding one coffee bean on a coffee plantation. These kids know how to get lost in the crowd."

"Why do you think he took it?" Mindy asked.

"The clothes in the suitcase must have looked pretty attractive," Warren pointed out. "He'll get good money for them."

"Boy, if Antonio had any idea what was *really* in there," K.J. observed, "he'd be set for life!"

Suddenly, a knock rattled the front door.

"I'm outta here," Mindy whispered. "I don't think I can take being around that Carlos guy anymore."

"I'm with you, Mindy," K.J. followed her from the living room. "He gives me the creeps."

The knock came again, louder this time. Ricardo opened the door.

Jeff gulped when he saw Carlos. His eyes

looked fierce, and he was holding a large box. Jeff was sure it was Mindy's case.

"Let's make this quick," Carlos snapped. "Where's the case?"

"We have some very bad news, señor." Ricardo looked frightened. "We were robbed by *gamines*. They stole the suitcase from my closet."

Carlos eyes flared with rage. "Don't lie to me! I want that case now."

Cold chills raced up Jeff's spine.

"Señor, we have no reason to lie," Ricardo pleaded. "We haven't gone to the police. We've done everything you asked."

A dark rage covered Carlos' face. "Everybody sit down. I'll search the house myself. If I find you are lying to me..." Carlos left his threat hanging as he left the living room.

Jeff could track Carlos's progress by the sounds. Things crashed to the floor in room after room as he continued down the hall. He heard him yell at Mindy and K.J. They ran out to join the others.

"I'm scared," Mindy cried, sitting near her brother.

"God will watch over us," Jeff quietly reminded her.

After about an hour, Carlos finally stomped into the living room, his suit rumpled and his face red. Angry eyes scanned them. "Lucky for you, I didn't find the case. And unlucky for you too."

Everyone sat still.

"I'm taking one of you hostage until I get the case."

Mindy cowered in the corner of the couch. K.J. didn't move.

Ricardo stood up. "Señor, my neighbor saw the kids who did it. Please give us more time. I promise I'll get the suitcase. There is no need to take a hostage."

Carlos paced the floor in silence. "This is your final chance," he said at last. "You have 48 hours. If you don't have it by midnight Monday, there will be no mercy."

"Gracias, señor," Ricardo said. "Gracias."

Carlos kicked the box from the doorway toward Mindy's feet. "Here! You can have this. It's useless to us."

Again, he glared at everyone in the room. His eyes were as cold as glaciers. "Remember, you have until Monday night." Carlos pointed a finger in Ricardo's face, then he stomped to the door and slammed it behind him.

"That was close," Ricardo whispered.

"Whew," Jeff gasped. "I think I'm breathing again."

Mindy opened the cardboard box. "At least I got my stuff back. Now maybe I'll have something clean to wear to church tomorrow." She pulled her suitcase out. "No wonder you got them confused, K.J. It looks identical, doesn't it?"

A half-smile crossed her face when she discovered everything was inside. "These clothes just don't look like they used to."

"What does that mean?" K.J. asked. "Did they change colors or something?"

"No. I think I'm the one who's changed," Mindy replied. "They're not as important to me as they were before. I'm going to leave some for your staff, Ricardo."

"I'm sure they would appreciate it."

"Great idea, Mindy," K.J. said sheepishly. "Maybe I'll give some of mine away too."

Warren laughed a little, pleased at their generosity. "Ricardo," he said, "how are we going to find Antonio?"

"We'll have to pay kids for information," Ricardo replied. "We'll do that after church tomorrow."

"Should we cancel the church meetings so we can do it first thing in the morning?" Warren asked.

"No." Ricardo shook his head. "God honors those who put Him first. I think we need to praise Him in worship first. And ask for His guidance and wisdom."

"You're right," Warren agreed. "You're absolutely right. We better get to bed then. Tomorrow is going to be a long day."

Jeff, Mindy, and K.J. filed into the little adobe church with Ricardo. They were going to share their testimonies, and K.J. was to film some interviews.

Warren had gone to speak in another church. Jeff felt privileged that Warren trusted him to lead the group in his absence. *Warren is like a good coach,* Jeff decided. *He likes to see the other players play.*

The worship songs were special to Jeff this morning. Though the words were in Spanish, he recognized the tunes and sang along quietly. The

Colombian believers worshipped with noise and passion, like a party to honor the Lord. Loud shouts and trills filled the little church.

When things calmed down, Ricardo introduced everyone.

Jeff walked forward. "We're glad to be here. Over the past few days, our hearts have melted with love for the children."

Jeff told of Roberto's conversion. Throughout the congregation, he heard sniffles. People everywhere were wiping their eyes.

After Jeff spoke, Mindy and K.J. gave their testimonies, told about the club, and explained their purpose for being there. Then, to Jeff's surprise, the pastor took a special offering for the work at the center. People gave joyfully. Some even danced their way down the aisle to put money in the basket.

Before dismissing everyone, the pastor invited people to stay and talk to the team. A number of young people gathered around Jeff, Mindy, and K.J. to hear more about the Reel Kids Club.

Suddenly there was a loud boom, followed by a terrifying rumble.

The pastor shouted, "Terremoto!"

Jeff recognized the Spanish word for *earthquake*. Several people bolted for the door. Others sought cover under the tables at the back of the church. Jeff looked around for K.J. and Mindy. He was relieved when he spotted them under a heavy table.

"Over here, Jeff!" Mindy cried, extending a trembling hand to him.

"I'm almost glad for our California earthquake training," Jeff said as he joined them.

Ricardo ran over, sliding under the table. "When the shaking is over, we'll head outside."

People continued to shout and scramble for shelter, though most had run out of the church. As he sat under the table, waiting for the shaking to stop, Jeff was reminded just how fragile life was. Things could be destroyed in a second.

When the first jolt was over, Jeff grabbed the others and made a run for it.

The crowd swelled outside. People flooded out of nearby buildings. Jeff, Mindy, K.J., and Ricardo were swept helplessly down the crowded street, trapped in the middle of a shoving, screaming throng of human bodies.

At the next rumble and shake, the street trembled and a loud, terrified wail rose from the crowd. Jeff couldn't believe his eyes. Bricks and stones rained down.

Ricardo moved closer. "Don't be afraid. This isn't a real bad earthquake."

"Not bad?" Mindy shrieked. "No matter how many I've been through, they never get easy."

"I have had better days too!" K.J. screamed as they ran.

They made their way to a park on the corner. Because it was an open area with nothing overhead to crash to the ground, it was filling with people.

They stopped near a panicked mother and four small children, who were all clambering to be held. By nodding and extending her arms, Mindy offered her help. She put her arm around the trembling mother, who finally relaxed her grip on her infant. Mindy held one child's hand and comforted the other.

K.J. sat down and leaned against a large tree trunk. Then, to Jeff's surprise, K.J. held out his hands to a curly-haired boy who looked about two years old. The boy hesitated a moment, his fingers in his mouth, then snuggled into K.J.'s lap.

Jeff smiled with pride.

K.J. pushed against the tree. "Do you think this will hold?"

"I think you're safe," Ricardo laughed.

"I hope Warren's okay," Jeff said. "Is the church sturdy?"

"Not really." Ricardo frowned. "He's speaking at one of the oldest churches in town. I hope he's okay."

"We have these in California all the time," Jeff commented as leaves fluttered from the tree. "Maybe it's because I'm not familiar with this place, but this earthquake is scary," he admitted.

Mindy looked over and nodded. "I feel so insecure when the ground shakes."

People stood, stunned and silent among the flowers and shrubs in the park.

"Can anything else happen on this trip?" K.J. wondered aloud.

"I hope not," Mindy muttered, holding the child.

Even though the ground was still rumbling, a few people began leaving.

"Can we go now?" K.J. asked.

Ricardo put his hand up. "Let's wait a little longer. The worst shakes usually come at the end, and that's when the buildings collapse. These stucco buildings can fold in on themselves like ruined cakes."

Chapter 9

Wounded

Are there usually aftershocks here?" Mindy asked.

"It's probably the same as California," Ricardo replied. "You never know for sure. You hope there aren't, but aftershocks sometimes continue for days."

"I hate them," Mindy muttered. "They can be worse than the earthquake."

The ground rumbled again, followed by a loud boom. Mindy pulled the little one closer with one hand and held on. She looked brave, but Jeff knew better. Her other hand kept clawing into his side.

"Take it easy, Sis. We'll be all right," he said as he wiped tears from the little girl's eyes.

"How big do you think it was?" K.J. asked, looking toward Ricardo.

"It couldn't have been more than a five. Anything more than that brings buildings down."

"Really?" Mindy buried her head between the children.

"There's not much difference between your earthquakes and ours," Ricardo said. "The difference is in the way our buildings are constructed. You have strict building codes. We don't. Many more people are injured here."

"I think I'm going to sleep outside tonight." Mindy sighed.

An hour or so passed. The toddler on K.J.'s lap squealed when he saw a frantic-looking man enter the park. The young mother beside Mindy ran to embrace the man. After thanking Jeff, Mindy, and K.J. for their help, he led his family away. By this time, most of the crowd had left.

Jeff looked at his watch. It was almost four o'clock.

"I wonder if Warren is okay," K.J. said.

Jeff nodded his concern and scanned the area around him. Within minutes, Jeff saw Warren picking his way over debris on the other side of the street.

"There he is!" Jeff yelled, pointing.

Everyone looked in the direction Jeff had indicated, and K.J. whistled to get Warren's attention.

Instantly, Warren spotted them and jogged over.

"Boy, am I glad to see you guys!" he said, grabbing them all in one big Texas hug.

"We're glad to see you!" Mindy said. "Was everybody okay where you were?"

"For the most part. A few people suffered minor cuts or bruises, but most of them were already outside when it happened. It was the ones inside who got injured."

"Where were you?" Jeff asked, thankful that Warren was okay.

"I was inside talking to people."

"You look fine," Ricardo observed. "How is that possible?"

"Well, it was close—I almost got a beam in the head." Warren gave them a wry smile. "But the centers, Ricardo. Are they okay?"

"I'm sure everything is fine at the main house," Ricardo said. "It's a one story and built pretty solid. We've come through some pretty good shakes in that house." He winked and whispered to Mindy, "I can't help thinking those stained glass angels have something to do with it."

She laughed and nodded her head.

"Well, what'll we do now?" Jeff asked.

Ricardo looked at his watch. "I'm starved! There's a food stand around the corner. Let's see if they're open. Then we'll look for Antonio. Time is running out."

After a few tacos, everyone felt better. Mindy tried to stifle a yawn.

Ricardo laughed. "You missed your siesta today, didn't you?"

"Well, who could sleep with all that shaking?" Mindy yawned again. "Earthquakes have a way of messing up schedules. We should have been looking for Antonio."

Ricardo was fingering his mustache when he suddenly jumped to his feet. "I've got an idea!"

"We'll do whatever you ask. Our lives are on the line here," K.J. said.

"We need to talk to Roberto!" Ricardo's eyes were bright. "Until yesterday, he lived on the streets. He'll know where to look."

Jeff lit up, nodding his head in approval.

"Let's head to the center," Ricardo went on. "Besides, I'm anxious to see if everyone is okay."

"Great idea." Jeff started walking in the direction of the center. "I miss Roberto already. It'll be good to see him. And Flora too, of course."

Mindy giggled to herself. "Of course, Jeff."

Jeff ignored her.

The team hurried along with Ricardo, and Jeff spotted Flora nearly a block before they arrived at the center. "Look! There's Flora. She's sweeping up glass."

The damage became more apparent as they got closer. The structure looked intact, but several windows were broken. The sign from the front of the building had fallen.

"Roberto's helping too," Jeff pointed out.

Flora waved. Jeff and K.J. raced to her side. Roberto was so excited to see them that he dropped his broom.

"Are you guys okay?" Jeff asked.

"It was pretty scary for a while," Flora said. "Most of the windows are broken. A few things fell off kitchen shelves, but we're fine."

Ricardo headed inside to survey the damages, and Jeff picked up the broom to help Flora. "No one was hurt?"

"No," Flora said. "God protected us. Most of the staff and kids were on the way back from church."

"Would you ask Roberto how he's doing?"

"Sure." Flora smiled.

Roberto grinned while Flora translated Jeff's question.

"He says he's fine," Flora put Roberto's words into English. "He enjoyed the party last night and said that yesterday was the happiest day of his life."

"Ricardo needs to talk to him," Jeff said, "to see if he can help us find Antonio."

Roberto nodded his approval and went looking for Ricardo. Jeff knew he had understood without translation.

"We'll help clean up this glass," Jeff offered.

Mindy and K.J. grabbed brooms and started sweeping. The sidewalks were full of people cleaning up the aftereffects of the earthquake.

"I'm glad it doesn't get hot around here," K.J. said.

"Why's that?" Flora asked.

"You guys sure keep us working a lot!" He laughed.

Mindy punched K.J. in the arm, and Flora swept at his leg with her broom.

When they finished cleaning out front, Jeff and

K.J. walked on each side of Flora as they headed inside. They nearly tripped over themselves trying to open the door for her. It slammed in Mindy's face, but she just shook her head and giggled.

They met Ricardo at the door.

"Roberto says Antonio hangs out on Calle 85," Ricardo told them. "That's an expensive shopping district. Taxis constantly drop people off at the popular night clubs. We'll start there."

Jeff thought for a moment. "Isn't that where we first saw him? That's where we gave him some money."

Ricardo nodded. "Kids hang out everywhere. They have their own turf, but they'll go anywhere for money."

Suddenly, they felt another sharp rumble. Mindy grabbed Jeff. K.J. started to run outside, but he stopped in his tracks when the shaking did.

"It's okay," Ricardo assured them. "That one seemed harmless enough." He turned to Mindy, Jeff, and K.J. "We've got some time tonight. I think we should stick together and walk the streets."

Jeff yawned at the breakfast table, causing a chain reaction. Everyone else yawned too. They had searched the streets until 11 the night before, but had come up empty. Today they planned to combine searching with videotaping.

"I think we should go to Calle 85 and wait at one of the taxi stops for a while," Jeff suggested.

"That's a good idea." Warren set his blue coffee

cup down. "I need you to help me with a decision, though. I'm scheduled to teach at the university the next three mornings. I'm debating whether I should cancel. What do you think?"

Ricardo looked up. "It seems a shame to waste this opportunity. I'll go with the kids to find Antonio. You'll be done after lunch, won't you?"

"I could meet you at Calle 85 around one. Is that okay with you guys?" Warren looked at each of them.

"Go ahead," Jeff said. "Fear shouldn't rule us. God will help us find Antonio."

"You're right, Jeff," Warren agreed. "Let's pray together. God knows where Antonio is."

Everyone bowed their heads, and Warren looked over at Mindy. "Why don't you lead us?"

Mindy waited a moment. "Lord Jesus," she finally began, "thanks for protecting us. Thanks for getting my suitcase back—and my clothes with it. Please help us find Antonio before it's too late. Amen."

"I'm sick of green and white taxis," Mindy whined. "We've been here for hours."

"Warren will be here soon." Jeff's watch indicated it was almost one. "Then we'll figure out a different strategy."

"We haven't seen many street kids today," K.J. said. "Don't they come out in the daytime?"

Ricardo lifted his hand to shield himself from the blistering sun. "They're usually here day or night. Maybe the earthquake damaged the old buildings they hang out in. They could be digging things out or sleeping in the park."

"Maybe we should look there," Mindy suggested.

"Let's wait for Warren first." Ricardo pulled on his mustache. "We'll begin again this afternoon."

Throughout the afternoon, the team searched everywhere. When they reached the park around dinnertime, Jeff sat down, too tired to look anymore. "We wasted an entire day looking for Antonio," he sighed.

K.J. held up his camera. "Not entirely. I got some great footage of you talking to kids."

Ricardo scratched his head. "We must have given away 50 dollars today. No one seems to know anything about Antonio."

"Tonight I'm hiding if we don't find that suitcase," Mindy said. "Those guys are gonna have their guns blazing!"

K.J. laughed nervously. "Where are you going to hide, Mindy?"

"I don't know." Mindy glared at him. "Maybe Ricardo's friend Franco will take us on a long plane ride."

"That's not a bad idea," Ricardo said. "We just might consider it."

"Or we could catch a jet home," Mindy added.

"Aw, come on, Min." Jeff gave her a little hug. "We can't quit now. God will come through. You wait and see."

Another tremor hit, but it was much milder. Everyone's eyes got bigger, but no one moved.

"Either the tremors are getting lighter," K.J. muttered, "or that was my stomach. I'm starving."

Ricardo nodded. "Let's go to the house. The cook said he'd have dinner ready when we got home."

After dinner, the door burst open and Flora ran in. Her face was red. She'd obviously run all the way from the center.

"Something dreadful has happened!" she screamed, trying to catch her breath.

Everyone jumped to their feet.

"Antonio's been shot!"

Chapter 10

Broken Hearts

"What happened?" Mindy cried.

"Just a few minutes ago, one of our kids ran into the center." Flora's breaths came in gasps. "He said Antonio's gang was in a major fight with another gang. If we hurry, we can get there before..."

"Before what?" Jeff asked.

"He might die." Flora's eyes brimmed with tears. "The boy said it looked pretty bad. Let's hurry. It's not far."

"Everybody in the van!" Ricardo ordered.

They rushed to the blue van, and Ricardo sped to the area where the fight had taken place. Jeff prayed silently. He knew K.J. and Mindy were doing the same.

Ricardo turned down the street. Jeff saw a crowd of kids standing around a crumpled figure on the sidewalk.

Mindy pulled on her ponytail. "I prayed we would find him. But I didn't want it this way."

"Hold on, Mindy," Warren whispered. "We don't know if it's over yet."

Ricardo screeched to a halt at the edge of the crowd. Jeff threw the door open, jumped out, and ran toward Antonio. The others were close behind, pushing their way through the gawking bystanders.

"Oh, it's only a *gamine*," Jeff heard someone in the crowd say. Jeff felt an impulse to tear the guy's head off for saying that, but he ignored it. He realized God didn't know these boys as "street kids," but as His kids—and that's what mattered.

Antonio's frightened gang stood in a huddle and strained to see over the crowd. Jeff wanted to comfort them all, but he knew there wasn't time. He rushed to Antonio's side.

Antonio lay on his stomach with a gunshot wound clearly visible in his back. Jeff stepped in the pool of blood to check Antonio's pulse. "I don't think he's breathing," he said in alarm.

The others were quickly by his side.

"What should we do?" Mindy cried. "Did anyone call an ambulance?"

Flora removed her jacket and pressed it against Antonio's wound to try to stop the bleeding. "He needs a doctor," her voice was low. "We've got to get him to a doctor."

Just then, a policeman strolled up. In broken English, he asked, "Do you know this boy?" He turned to the crowd. "Does anyone know this boy?" he repeated.

Jeff couldn't stand the silence. "I do, sir!" he yelled. "I do!"

"Then get him to a hospital," the policeman snapped.

Jeff couldn't believe it. Didn't anybody care for these kids more than that?

Ricardo turned to Warren. "I'll get the van while you carry Antonio. The hospital is only a few streets away."

Carefully, Jeff and Warren turned Antonio over. Antonio moaned softly, and Jeff could see that his eyes had rolled back in his head. He prayed earnestly.

Warren lifted him gently and hurried to the van. "Let's go. We don't have much time."

Warren laid Antonio across the seat, and Ricardo hurried everyone inside. Flora jumped in last.

Jeff couldn't believe it. They had searched for Antonio all day, and now he lay bleeding, maybe dying, in the van. The suitcase didn't matter anymore. What mattered was Antonio's life.

Ricardo sped the van through the streets and finally screeched to a stop at the emergency entrance.

"Flora! I'm going inside!" Ricardo shouted as he jumped out and hailed a nearby nurse. "Park the van!"

Jeff slid the door open for Warren, who carried Antonio inside and laid him on a waiting stretcher.

"This boy's been shot!" Ricardo cried in Spanish. "He's been shot!"

Jeff watched as two nurses rushed Antonio away on the stretcher. Ricardo and Warren went with him. Jeff stood gazing at the door they disappeared through. He became aware of at least a dozen other people waiting to be helped. In spite of the crowd, he felt totally alone.

He glanced around the waiting area. It looked pretty much like any other hospital he'd ever seen— plain white walls with a few pictures. Signs were posted everywhere, in Spanish of course. Nurses and attendants rushed around. Wheelchairs and stretchers were stacked along one corner of the entrance.

Flora, K.J., and Mindy appeared at the entrance.

Mindy approached Jeff shakily. "Do you think he's going to make it?"

Jeff saw her brown eyes filling with tears. He hugged her gently and realized this time he needed a hug as badly as she did.

"I hope so, Sis. I hope so."

They waited for what seemed like hours. And then Ricardo and Warren returned.

"They've taken him to the operating room," Ricardo reported. "The doctor said the bullet entered Antonio's back and came out his stomach. He wasn't sure how much damage they'd find inside, but there's a lot of blood loss. The doctor didn't have much hope."

"Let's pray." Jeff looked at his friends. "That's the hope we have for Antonio now."

The hours passed too slowly. They stood. They sat. They paced. They drank coffee and soda. They prayed. They paced some more.

"You know," Jeff said, "this might be God's way of answering our prayer. He wants to touch Antonio."

K.J. kicked at a chair. "It's almost 10 o'clock. I hope he regains consciousness before midnight. He needs to tell us about the suitcase, or we're all dead."

Mindy stared angrily at him. "All you care about is your own hide, K.J.! You should be caring about what Ricardo and Warren are finding out from the doctors!"

"It's not that I don't care," K.J. protested. "But I'm not ready to die either."

Jeff stood up. "We've got two hours before the deadline. There's no way he'll wake up by then."

"You will have to hide somewhere." Flora's voice was flat with exhaustion.

"What about you?" Jeff looked at her in concern. "Nobody will be safe if the drug cartel goes on a killing spree."

K.J. laughed nervously. "Yeah. We might as well wait here. We may all need a hospital room soon."

Warren slowly walked up to the group with Ricardo. "The doctor said Antonio will be coming out of surgery soon. He lost a lot of blood. He's got a better chance now, but he won't be conscious for hours."

"What about the suitcase?" K.J. asked.

"Antonio won't be able to help us now," Ricardo said.

"What about the gang?" Jeff looked from Ricardo to Warren.

"We don't have time to find them tonight," Warren replied.

"What are we going to do?" they all asked at once.

Ricardo wiped perspiration from his forehead. "Warren and I will go back to the house to wait for Carlos. We'll plead for another 24 hours. I think you guys should stay here with Antonio."

"Be careful," was all Jeff knew to say.

It was one o'clock, and Jeff was anxious to know what was going on back at the house. He tapped his foot nervously. Mindy was sleeping in a chair, while K.J. paced the floor. Flora had walked back to the center.

"I'm going to go find the doctor." Jeff stood in exasperation. "I need to know if there's been any change. I can't stand this waiting!"

"I'll stay here with Mindy," K.J. muttered.

Before Jeff got out of the waiting area, Warren and Ricardo rushed in. "Where's Flora?" Ricardo asked, out of breath.

"She went back to the center," Jeff answered. "Are we doomed?"

"Not yet," Ricardo said. "I know it sounds like a miracle, but Carlos believed my story. I invited him to the hospital to prove it. He's given us until Antonio wakes up to return the suitcase."

Mindy woke up in time to hear the last few sentences. "Carlos is coming here?"

"That's better than the other option, isn't it?" K.J. said sarcastically.

"I don't know," Mindy cried. "I don't want to be here when Carlos shows up!"

"We need to stay here," Jeff said, "for Antonio. The doctor will allow two of us to be in the room with him."

"And what about Carlos?" Mindy asked, her eyes wide awake now.

Ricardo smiled at her. "He won't come until Antonio is conscious. He's calling the hospital every hour. He's going to tell the receptionist that Antonio is his nephew."

"His nephew!" K.J. laughed. "And I'm his grandfather!"

"Jeff and K.J. will stay tonight," Warren said. "We'll switch tomorrow."

"Okay with us," Jeff said. "Go get some sleep, Mindy."

Jeff woke up in the middle of a dream.

After his eyes adjusted to the light, he realized he was in the hospital room with Antonio. K.J. was curled up in a big chair, sound asleep. Jeff's heart sunk when he saw that Antonio was still unconscious.

Jeff tapped the leg of K.J.'s chair. "K.J., wake up."

K.J. opened one eye. His face was embossed with the same pattern that covered the vinyl chair. "What's up, man?"

"It's nine o'clock."

"So?" K.J. said with a yawn.

"I just had a wild dream."

"And you woke me to tell me that? Agghhhh! Okay, okay, what happened?"

"I didn't get to finish it, but I saw Antonio walking around. He had a big smile on his face."

"In this dream of yours, did you find out if we lived or not?"

"No. But I think God gave it to me as a sign that everything is going to be okay."

"Well, buddy, I hope all your dreams come true."

"Lets pray for it to happen."

Jeff and K.J. walked over to Antonio's bed. They placed their hands on Antonio's head, and Jeff began to pray. "Father, heal Antonio. Help him to see You as his real Father. Amen."

K.J. and Jeff were silent, watching Antonio intently. Minutes passed.

"Look, K.J.!" Jeff whispered hoarsely. "I think he's moving. This is unbelievable! All right, God!"

Chapter 11

Escape

Jeff and K.J. stood beside the bed. Antonio's fingers twitched slightly, but his eyes were still closed.

"He's going to live!" Jeff cried.

"He's a pretty tough guy," K.J. whispered, amazed.

"He's had to be to endure what he has in life."

"I hope Carlos doesn't show up now." K.J. frowned. "We still need to find the suitcase."

"Don't worry about that yet. First, Antonio needs to know we care about him."

K.J. grinned. "Hey! Maybe we should tell the doctor Carlos isn't really Antonio's uncle. We can let him know Carlos wants to hurt him."

"Not a bad idea. Maybe the doctor would help us buy some time. But we can't get him to lie for us."

K.J. grinned again. "Maybe the nurse could hold the doctor's calls. Then Carlos couldn't get through, and the doctor wouldn't have to lie."

"What have we got to lose?"

Ricardo and Mindy walked in.

"Any changes?" Mindy asked.

Jeff told them his dream about Antonio being well and happy—and that Antonio had moved just seconds ago. Then they discussed K.J.'s idea.

"What do you think, Ricardo?" Jeff asked.

"We need to be careful about the doctor," he cautioned. "I'll go talk to him and see what he says."

K.J., Mindy, and Jeff waited an hour before Ricardo returned. They had all watched Antonio, but he hadn't moved again.

"I had to tell the doctor the whole story to convince him to help us," Ricardo began. "He agreed to have his nurse hold any calls from Carlos until four this afternoon. He's even willing to transfer Antonio to another hospital if things get bad."

"That's great, Ricardo!" Jeff said.

"Warren is at the university," Ricardo added. "But we can call him there if we need him. I'm going to the center." He turned to Mindy. "Did you want to stay or come with me?"

"I think I'll stay, Ricardo," Mindy replied. "Just in case Antonio wakes up."

"What if Carlos figures out what's going on and

comes down here?" Jeff asked.

"Just pray Antonio is sleeping if he drops in," was Ricardo's reply.

Jeff dozed off for a while. About four o'clock, he stretched, yawned, and opened his eyes.

"About time you woke up," K.J. said. "Warren stopped in, but he didn't want to wake you. He took Mindy to the center, but they should be back soon."

"How close are we to getting the footage we need?" Jeff stifled another yawn.

"We need a few more shots," K.J. said. "I want to do some interviews with kids like Roberto. What a story!"

Out of the corner of his eye, Jeff saw something move. He quickly turned toward Antonio, whose eyelids were fluttering slightly. Then he moaned.

"Should we call the nurse?" K.J. cried.

"Let's give him another few minutes."

Jeff and K.J. watched Antonio intently. It looked like he was trying to open his eyes. Behind them, Ricardo, Warren, and Mindy walked in.

"Hurry," Jeff whispered, motioning them to come close. "He's waking up."

Ricardo leaned over the bed. "Antonio," he called gently, "Antonio, wake up."

Antonio peeked at Ricardo, then at Jeff.

"What happened?" he muttered.

They all squealed and jumped in unison.

A nurse rushed in. "What's all the noise about?" she said sharply. "This is a hospital!" Then she saw

Antonio. She checked his pulse then hurried to get the doctor.

The doctor came in and shined a tiny flashlight into Antonio's eyes. He moaned a complaint.

"This is a miracle," the doctor said in broken English.

"I never thought he'd make it. That bullet didn't hit any major organs, but we had a lot of cleaning up to do in there. He lost a lot of blood."

Everyone laughed with joy.

The doctor pulled out smelling salts and held them under Antonio's nose. "This will wake him up. I'll leave it with you. Make him sniff it every 15 minutes. I'll check back later."

"Thanks, doctor," Mindy said.

The doctor started to walk out, then he turned back. "By the way, Carlos Lopez hasn't called back. Maybe he will leave you alone."

"We hope so," Ricardo sighed.

Antonio's eyes opened when they used the smelling salts again. Jeff didn't like the anger he saw in them.

Antonio started mumbling something.

"What's he saying?" Jeff asked.

"I think he wants us to leave him alone," Ricardo said. "He's not interested in God or us."

Jeff moved closer, looking into his eyes. "We care about you, Antonio. We're glad you're still alive."

The look on Antonio's face got colder, but Jeff didn't give up. "We brought you here after you were shot. We're praying for you to get well."

Antonio muttered what sounded like Spanish

swear words and turned his face away.

"What did he say?" Jeff wanted to know.

"I can't tell you all of it," Ricardo said. "But he wants us to leave."

Jeff was frustrated. God had broken through in Roberto's heart. He knew there had to be a key to Antonio's heart as well.

"Let me tell you one more thing," Jeff spoke quietly to Antonio, smiling. "No matter what you say or how you try to hurt us, we're going to love you."

Antonio scoffed and shut his eyes.

"I had a dream about you last night," Jeff continued. "You were a happy kid again."

Antonio grimaced with pain and buried his face in the pillow.

Ricardo motioned everyone to step out. They went to the waiting room where he faced them. "We have to make a decision."

Everyone looked puzzled.

"Tonight is the final deadline," Ricardo went on. "I'm going to have to talk to Antonio about the suitcase. It'll probably make him mad, but our friend Carlos may do more than make him mad."

"What if he denies it?" Jeff asked. "He's not in a very good mood."

"Well, I can't blame him for not being in a good mood," Ricardo said. "But we don't have a choice. I have to ask him about the suitcase."

Everyone nodded in agreement.

"I'll be right back. Please pray."

After only a few minutes, Ricardo returned. The expression on his face indicated it hadn't gone well.

"What'd he say?" Mindy asked quickly.

"He got angry. He didn't deny or admit it. He just got angry. Finally, the nurse asked me to leave."

"What now?" Jeff was at a loss. "We're really in a jam."

Suddenly, the doctor rushed up. "Mr. Lopez just called. He's very upset. He said he's coming to the hospital."

"What are you going to do?" Ricardo looked at the doctor.

The doctor frowned. "I don't know, but you don't have much time. If I were you, I'd get out of here."

Hurrying to the van, Jeff knew they had to do something—fast. K.J. and Mindy climbed in, but Warren and Ricardo pulled Jeff aside.

Ricardo took a deep breath. "The drug cartel has lost all patience, and I am worried for your lives. We need to get you guys out of here."

"What do you mean, get us out of here?" Jeff asked.

"I've talked to Franco," Ricardo replied. "Remember, my friend the pilot? He's agreed to fly you to our center in Sitka."

"I'm confused," Jeff said. "Sitka? Alaska?"

"There's a Sitka in Colombia too," Ricardo was quick to point out. "It's not far from here by plane. We were planning for you to visit there anyway. And for now it's a safe place."

"What would we do there?" Jeff asked.

"About 40 kids who used to live on the streets of Bogota live on a farm there," Roberto continued. "They have all accepted Christ as their Savior and are learning more about Him. You can get some great interviews. It'll be fun. And...it will buy us more time."

"Are you coming, Warren?" Jeff asked.

"I can't." Warren shook his head. "The plane is a four-seater. I'll stay at the university for a night or two. I'll help Ricardo with the suitcase problem." He put his hand on Jeff's shoulder and looked into his eyes. "I can't allow you to be exposed to any more danger. Besides," he added, lightening up, "you guys wanted a plane ride."

"Yeah. A plane ride would be fun. And meeting other kids like Roberto sounds terrific. But not on these terms." Questions swirled in Jeff's mind. "What about you, Ricardo? And Flora and the rest of the staff? Will they be safe?"

Ricardo smiled. "You have a big heart, Jeff Caldwell. But you can't protect us all. We'll probably be safer if you guys leave for a while. We'll tell Carlos you're touring Colombia. And we promise to call you the minute it's safe to come back."

"What about Antonio?" Jeff asked.

"He'll be safe in the hospital," Ricardo answered. "He might be the only one who knows where the suitcase is, and that's enough for the drug cartel to keep him alive."

"Then why aren't we safe?" Jeff wanted to know. "Hurting us wouldn't help them find the suitcase any faster."

"I'll be straight with you, Jeff." Ricardo frowned. "Besides murder, the drug cartel is notorious for kidnapping. They use it as a bargaining tool."

"I'm getting the picture." Jeff nodded his head.

"When would we leave?"

Ricardo checked his watch. "Franco will meet you at the airport in two hours."

Chapter 12

Emergency

Once inside the van, Warren and Jeff explained the whole situation to K.J. and Mindy. Mindy looked frightened, but K.J. got excited.

"All right!" K.J. exclaimed. "I'll do some video footage from the plane. Those mountains will look awesome from up there. I can get great shots of the city and the mountains."

Warren laughed out loud. "I hate to break up the fun," he said as they pulled up to the house, "but we need to hurry. Please pack light."

121

"What do you mean?" Mindy asked, jumping out of the van. "How long are we going to stay?"

"Well, we're scheduled to fly back to L.A. Friday morning," Warren answered. "This is Tuesday, so it won't be more than a day or two."

"Don't forget," K.J. put in, "I need two more shots of kids on the streets here. And we've got to get an interview with Roberto."

"We'll have time for that later," was all Warren said.

Cool winds refreshed Jeff's face as he stood at El Dorado Airport. He looked over the small Cessna airplane while K.J. filmed everything in sight. Franco made last-minute preparations for their flight.

Jeff was glad to see twin engines. Though it could have used a new paint job, the plane seemed solid.

"How long will take to get there?" Mindy asked.

Franco looked up from his work. "A couple of hours—if the winds are with us."

K.J. bounced over to Jeff. "Let's shoot you and Mindy describing the trip. It'll be a good opener for the interviews."

Jeff smiled and ran his fingers through his hair. He was always ready for an interview.

Franco called from near the wing, "We'll be ready for takeoff in ten minutes. Get your luggage over here by then."

K.J. positioned the camera. "Stand over here in front of the plane."

Jeff and Mindy stood near one of the engines. K.J. made small circles with his hand as a sign that the camera was rolling.

Clearing his throat, Jeff looked into the lens. "Today, we're going on a special trip to visit a center for homeless children. Shortly, you'll meet kids rescued from life on the dangerous streets of Bogota. This home is sponsored by International Children's Centers.

"Bogota businessman Franco Juarez uses his personal plane and his free time to help homeless children. He flies kids away from life on the streets of Bogota to a rural area where they are loved and nurtured—perhaps for the first time in their lives."

K.J. held three fingers up and started counting down. "Cut."

Mindy was relieved the spot was over, even though her job was only to smile. She was much more comfortable with a computer in her lap than a camera in her face.

K.J. played it back on his camcorder screen. "This is excellent, you guys. The Cessna in the background is perfect."

Franco hurried over. "Okay. Time to load the luggage."

Suddenly, Jeff saw a black Rolls Royce heading toward them. "Uh, oh. What if it's Carlos? What'll we do?"

"Quick! Toss me your luggage!" K.J. cried.

The tinted windows made it impossible to see anyone inside the car.

K.J. tossed their bags in the cargo hold. They all held their breath.

Franco watched the car. "If it's him, we'll never get out of here."

Everyone waited. Mindy looked terrified. K.J. aimed his camera at the car and whispered out of the side of his mouth, "Whether I die now or in 80 years, I want to go with a camera in my hand. Bury me that way too, will ya?"

In spite of the danger, Jeff chuckled and bopped his buddy on the arm. He could always trust K.J. to lighten up any situation.

They all nearly collapsed with relief when the car drove right past them and pulled up beside a King Air jet on the runway.

"That was too scary!" Mindy cried.

K.J. stared at the people getting out. "No offense, Franco, but I wouldn't mind flying in that baby. Those things have all the perks anyone could want."

"I think you'll like my Cessna." Franco grinned. "Climb in. Let's get out of here before Carlos really does show up."

Sitting beside Franco, Jeff tightened his seat belt. He looked the instruments over carefully. K.J. and Mindy put their seat belts on as well. As always, K.J. held his camera.

The engines roared to life, and they were on their way. Takeoffs always made Jeff smile. He loved the way the thrust of the plane pressed his body back against his seat and the feeling of power as the small plane climbed into the air.

The setting sun made their takeoff even more perfect. As if they were watching fireworks, Jeff, Mindy, and K.J. oohed and aahed over the sight. The sky was streaked with shades of pink, lavender, and purple. The mountains' tall cliffs and rugged terrain reflected incredible colors.

K.J. gasped at what he saw through his camera lens. "Boy, I'm glad we got to do this. It's incredible!"

Mindy took a couple of deep breaths. "Are you sure we can make it over those tall mountains?"

Jeff gave her a thumbs up sign.

Higher and higher they soared. Jeff peeked over the wing at the city of Bogota and the mountains surrounding it. Beautiful skyrise buildings jutted up from the heart of the city. Modern technology was encircled by countless acres of coffee fields.

"Could we go around a couple of times?" Jeff asked. "This is really incredible."

Franco nodded in agreement and banked to the left.

"Can you find the center from up here, K.J.?" Jeff turned to his friend. "Try to zoom in on it."

"Way ahead of ya, buddy. Got it in my viewfinder."

After one complete turn, Franco climbed higher. "We'll have to go now. I need to follow my flight plan."

Everyone sat back. The plane shook slightly when they passed through mild turbulence. All they could see now were mountain peaks and canyons.

Franco turned to Jeff. "You want to do some flying?"

"Sure." He hesitated a bit. "But I've never done it before."

Mindy leaned forward. "I don't think that's a good idea."

"Don't worry, Mindy." Franco laughed. "I've got dual controls. I can take over if Jeff gets in trouble."

Franco showed Jeff what to do. When Franco finished his lesson, they were at 10,000 feet above sea level.

"All you're going to do is steer," Franco assured Jeff. "It's not hard."

Jeff put both hands on the rectangular-shaped wheel and tried to hold it steady. But the tiniest move caused the plane's wings to go up and down.

K.J. filmed Jeff at the controls. Mindy was sitting on her hands, bouncing slightly in her seat.

"This is great!" Jeff said. "It takes a few minutes to get the feel of it, though."

K.J. put down the camera when Franco took back the controls.

Mindy relaxed a little.

"Can I try flying on the way home?" K.J. asked.

Franco nodded and smiled, then he began his descent. He raised his voice a little. "You've heard of Colombian coffee, haven't you? Well, below us are endless stretches of coffee fields. It's quite a sight in the daylight."

"My parents drink Colombian coffee," Jeff said. "I'll never look at a can of it again without remembering this day."

K.J. pointed out the window. "Look! I think I see a guy waving at us from his burro!"

Everyone laughed.

"How big is Sitka?" Jeff asked Franco.

"Fairly small in population. It's a farming community—a great place to take *gamines*. I'm always amazed how fast they change as they relax and work with their hands every day."

"Do they go to school?" Mindy wanted to know.

"Ricardo makes sure the centers provide a full education program. But it costs 20 dollars in U.S money per month to house and educate each child."

"I'll be sure to write that into the video script." Mindy pulled out her notepad. "Some kids could even get together to send that much."

"Twenty dollars a month is all it takes?" Jeff almost couldn't believe it. "It's amazing that you can make such drastic changes in a child's life for the price of what dinner and a movie costs in America."

"American money goes a long ways in Colombia," Franco explained. "You must have noticed how cheap things were in the market-places."

He shifted in his pilot's chair. "The Sitka Center is a farm. They grow their own vegetables and raise animals for food, so that saves money too. And the staff and kids live much more simply than people do in America."

Franco pointed out in the distance. "We're getting close. If you look carefully, you can see Sitka right over there."

Jeff strained to see. Lights twinkled like small diamonds. A full moon squatted over the mountains, making it almost as bright as daylight.

Out of the corner of his eye, Jeff spotted what looked like a cloud. But as he continued to watch, he realized it was a small trail of smoke coming from the left engine.

"Franco! Look! I think the engine's on fire."

Franco's eyes swept back and forth along the instrument panel. A warning light began flashing.

"We're losing oil pressure in one engine!" Franco yelled. "We need to get on the ground. Fast!"

Jeff looked back to Mindy and K.J. and made a praying gesture with his hands.

The trail of smoke continued growing bigger by the second.

"Can we make it?" Jeff felt panic filling his body.

"I'm going for it," Franco replied tensely.

Jeff prayed with all his might, but he didn't feel like his prayers were leaving the airplane. He whispered quickly, "Lord Jesus, I stand against the enemy. We're safe in Your arms because we're in Your will. Please get us to the airport."

K.J. leaned forward. "Where's that big, fancy King Air jet when we need it?"

"Not funny," Mindy screamed.

Again, Jeff looked out. The engine spewed out large clouds of smoke. A flame flickered. As he watched, the flames grew and mingled with the smoke.

"Keep praying!" Franco cried. "We're almost there."

Jeff saw the lights of the airstrip. Though it looked close, they were still miles away.

Franco radioed the air traffic controller in the small tower straight ahead, advising them of their emergency.

Jeff reached back, taking Mindy's hand. Although she wasn't saying a word, he knew she was panicky. "We'll make it, Sis." He tried to keep his voice calm. "We'll make it."

Jeff looked out again. The amount of smoke told him the engine should have exploded in flames by now.

K.J. had his camera out, filming everything.

"Come on, baby," Franco urged his troubled plane. "You can make it."

The runway got closer. Jeff couldn't bear to look at the engine, but he couldn't keep his eyes off it either. Dark, billowing clouds poured from the engine.

It could explode at any second.

Chapter 13

Kidnapped

Jeff's eyes were glued to the approaching airstrip. He watched an old fire truck pull out and speed to the runway. It was strange to think that the truck was pulling out for them.

"Not much farther!" Franco cried.

Jeff prayed harder. All of a sudden, he felt at peace. His body relaxed, and he somehow knew they would be okay. *This must be "the peace that passes all understanding" the Bible talks about,* he thought.

The engine was clearly visible in the bright

moonlight, and he watched the clouds of smoke get smaller by the second. God had answered their prayers.

Franco didn't have time to look. He was at 200 feet and straight in line with the runway.

Mindy squeezed the blood out of Jeff's hand. K.J. filmed the landing.

"Hang on," was all Franco said.

At last, Jeff heard the sweet sound of rubber meeting concrete. They all cheered.

"As soon as we stop, get away from the plane immediately," Franco ordered. "The engine could still explode."

As they taxied down the runway, a man on the ground signaled where to park. K.J. filmed the old fire truck speeding toward them.

Franco taxied to a stop, and a man in an old uniform instantly doused the engine with fire retardant. Spotlights were aimed at their plane.

Mindy gasped for air. Jeff took a deep breath and sent a little smile upward. Franco pulled the door open as fast as he could. One by one, they scrambled onto the tarmac.

Jeff was glad to be on solid earth.

Kneeling to kiss the ground, K.J. threw his hands in the air and shouted, "Thank You, Father!" When he got up, he put his arm around Jeff's shoulder. "Well, that was awful. But I did get some unbelievable footage. We should seriously think about making a movie."

Jeff and Mindy both shook their heads.

Franco stood quietly beside them, watching the fireman finish his job. "I'm so sorry," he said. "I've never had that happen before. My mechanic always checks the engine out."

"We're getting used to this," Jeff said.

"Speak for yourself, big brother," Mindy put in, still breathing unevenly.

Jeff saw a large man in blue slacks and a red sweater running toward them. He looked terrified.

"I'm so glad you're safe," he said, clasping Franco's hand. He turned to the team.

"So are we!" Mindy cried.

"This is David," Franco introduced the man. "He runs the center here in Sitka. And David, this is Jeff, Mindy, and K.J."

They all shook hands as Franco disappeared to examine the still-smoking engine.

"That was a close one," Jeff sighed.

"I saw the fire truck pull out of the hangar and wondered what was going on," David said. "I wasn't sure if it was your plane or not."

"Unfortunately, it was." Mindy rolled her eyes.

"The important thing is that you're safe." David smiled. "I'll have you at our center in a few minutes. We're not far from the airport."

"That's good. I'm exhausted," Mindy said. "I can't take this excitement. I'm ready for bed."

The fireman carried the luggage out, placing it on the runway. Amazingly, it was neither scorched nor wet.

Franco walked over. "David, can you take care of these guys? I'm going to stay here for a while. I need to find out what happened and get it fixed. I'll call for a ride later."

"Certainly," David replied.

The Wednesday morning sun was bright. Jeff had slept well. He looked forward to meeting some of the kids. But first he decided to walk and explore the center while he prayed.

Out the front door he saw a peaceful scene. Fences held horses and cows in separate fields. Chickens, geese, and an old billy goat roamed the property.

He passed a well-kept garden full of ripe vegetables and a small orchard of fruit trees. After walking a ways, he glanced back at the large, white farmhouse. *The perfect place to raise kids,* he thought. *Especially kids who have never known a home.*

David had given them a brief tour the night before. He told them the farmhouse housed about 20 kids in six bedrooms. Two bedrooms were used for visiting staff and guests. The farm fit nicely into Sitka's rural community.

The morning air felt good. Sitka's altitude wasn't nearly as high as Bogota's, which made breathing easier. Jeff heard the breakfast bell ring. With his stomach growling, he hurried toward the large dining room.

As he entered, he saw kids pouring out of the bedrooms. Chatting and laughing, they scrambled for a place at the breakfast table. There was a feeling of family about this place.

Jeff couldn't believe how young the kids were. The older ones couldn't have been over twelve. A few four- or five-year-olds tagged along, holding the hand of an older child.

Mindy and K.J. appeared, followed by two little ones. David was in the kitchen with an apron around his middle. Jeff scanned the room looking for Franco. He was anxious to find out what had gone wrong with the plane.

Just then, Franco strode in. He ruffled heads of hair and tickled small bellies all the way. Clearly, all the kids loved Franco.

David prayed for the food, then introduced the Reel Kids. The children applauded. Jeff thought these kids seemed different than the ones they had met in Bogota. Happier. More like children. It didn't take long for Mindy and K.J. to be surrounded. Wherever they went, they drew children like a magnet.

Franco joined Jeff and David.

"Did you find out what happened with the engine?" Jeff asked.

Franco took a sip from his coffee cup. "Ahhh. Colombian coffee!" He set the cup down. "Yes. One of the oil line fittings sprung a leak. We don't need to replace the whole line, but we're trying to locate a fitting."

"Do you think you'll find one here in Sitka?" David asked.

Franco finished a big bite of toast. "We're going to check the parts stores today, but as you know they've got a limited selection."

David smiled as he took a big sip from his cup. "We'd love to have you stay as long as you like. The children love company."

Jeff put down his fork. "Thanks for your hospitality, but we'll only be able to stay a day—two at the most."

"I understand you need to get back." David nodded. "I've asked the kids to be ready to do filming today. They're excited about having their pictures taken. Oh, and be sure you talk to a girl named Laura."

Jeff, Mindy, and K.J. interviewed kids all day. The little ones came by, giggled in the background, and waited their turn to sit on the old wooden chair K.J. used as a set. K.J. ran the camera while Mindy took notes as fast as her fingers could fly across her laptop computer. David translated.

Sitting on the porch with Jeff, nine-year-old Laura had waited for hours for her turn. Jeff looked into the camera and began, "Today, we're glad to have Laura with us. She is going to tell us about herself."

"My mom died right after I was born," Laura spoke quietly. "My dad was very poor."

David translated.

"My father used drugs. He spent all our money. When I was three, he forced me to go out and sell anything I could find."

Tears filled Mindy's eyes.

"My father hated me. He beat me just because I was a girl. He said I had brought shame to him because he wanted a boy."

Jeff pulled the microphone back to ask a question. "How did you end up at this center?"

"I couldn't take the beatings anymore. I started to fight back. One day, my father got very violent and ordered me to leave. I ended up on the streets with a gang of kids. We did anything we could to get money. A woman named Flora found me in an alley. She took me back to the center."

The camera panned back to Jeff. "And what happened when you came to the center?"

"For the first time in my life, I felt like someone liked me. I was accepted. They gave me food when I was hungry. They gave me a bed to sleep in."

Mindy's typing stopped. She got up and walked away because she was crying too hard.

"I want to grow strong in my faith so I can be like Flora," Laura continued. "I want to help other kids. They need to know about Jesus. I want to tell them."

With tears in his eyes, Jeff looked straight into the camera. "Here at Sitka's International Children's Center, you've met Laura. In closing, I want to raise a question that's troubled me since I arrived."

He paused. "What if there were no center here? What if there were no Davids, Ricardos, or Floras? Where would the Lauras be?"

K.J. put up his fingers again, counting down. "Cut."

Jeff hugged Laura.

K.J. walked over and reached for her hand. "Thanks, Laura. That was excellent. We hope it helps many more kids like you."

Laura nodded and smiled a smile that lit up her face.

Mindy came back and gently folded her arms around Laura. They hugged and cried. At that moment, Jeff was grateful he had given his life to serve Jesus. Nothing felt better than helping people in trouble.

Jeff looked at his watch. It was close to four o'clock.

"No word on the plane, David?" Jeff asked.

"Nothing."

"Nothing from Ricardo either? I'm dying to know what's happening with the suitcase."

David shrugged his shoulders.

"I'm glad you're so hospitable," Jeff added. "Looks like we'll be staying another day. But we have to head back tomorrow since we leave for home on Friday."

Suddenly, a staff member ran out, calling for David. She looked frightened. Together, they hurried inside.

Jeff, Mindy, and K.J. sat on the porch for a few minutes playing with the kids. When David came running back out, he looked sick.

"What's wrong?" they all asked.

"I have two kinds of news. Good and not very good."

"What's the good news?" K.J. cautiously asked.

"Antonio's had a change of heart. He wants to talk to Jeff as soon as possible."

"That's great!" Mindy cried.

"What could be bad after that?" Jeff wanted to know.

David looked down at the ground, wiping his hands. "Ricardo said there's been a kidnapping. Two men in business suits kidnapped one of the staff from the center in Bogota."

"Who?" Jeff cried. "Who?"

"Flora."

Chapter 14

Desperation

Everyone was still, too stunned to move.

"I was afraid something would happen." Jeff stomped his foot. "Not Flora! I knew I shouldn't have left."

"There's nothing you could've done to stop it." David tried to calm Jeff down. "The drug cartel does anything they want."

"But why Flora?" K.J. asked. "She had nothing to do with any of this."

"No one knows." David shook his head.

"Probably just because she was there. They want the suitcase by three o'clock Thursday. If not, they said they'd kill her."

"No," Jeff moaned, "no."

"And Antonio?" Mindy asked quietly. "What about Antonio?"

"The doctor gave him sedatives to make him sleep better," David answered. "Ricardo said he woke up this morning totally different."

"That's amazing." Jeff couldn't believe what he was hearing.

"Ricardo said Antonio gets tears in his eyes from time to time."

"Did he confess to stealing the suitcase?" Jeff was hopeful.

"He won't talk to anyone but you," David repeated. "Ricardo wants you guys back as soon as possible—even if you have to take another plane."

"We've got to get hold of Franco!" K.J. jumped to his feet.

"Let's go find him." Jeff stood beside his friend.

Everyone followed David inside. David asked the staff to get the kids together to pray for Flora. He then picked up the phone, dialed, and spoke quickly in Spanish.

Jeff looked at his watch when David hung up. It was 4:30. "What did you find out?" he asked.

"Franco is in town looking for the part he needs."

"Should we go looking for him?"

"Yes," David replied. "Get your things together in case he's ready to go."

"I'll grab Franco's stuff too," K.J. offered.

David drove to both parts stores in town. The team scoured the streets of Sitka, but no one had seen Franco.

"We've checked everywhere," Jeff said, returning to the car. "I can't believe we can't find him in a town this small!"

"We'll find him," David said confidently. "I know we will."

After driving around for nearly an hour, David decided to try the airport. A few minutes later, Jeff was crawling out of the car when he heard Mindy scream. "Look! There he is—out by his plane."

They slammed the car doors and raced to him. Jeff got there first, and the story of all that had happened poured out.

"Do you think we can get out of here tonight?" Jeff asked.

Franco shook his head sadly. "I've tried everything. A friend is flying in a part for me, but he won't be here until six o'clock tomorrow morning."

"That's cutting it close," Jeff groaned. "They said they'd kill Flora by three o'clock."

Franco looked depressed. "I've even tried to borrow a fitting, but none of these planes are like mine. Most of them need repair too."

"Can we take another flight?" Mindy suggested.

"The only scheduled flight leaves here at noon every day," Franco replied. "We have no choice but to stay."

"Can we drive?" Jeff pleaded.

Franco looked at his watch. "It's a very dangerous

ride over the mountains. If I get that part in the morning, we'll be there quicker by plane."

Jeff couldn't believe it. He didn't want Flora held by those evil men for a moment longer. He hated to think what they might do to her. He didn't even know if Antonio would tell them where the suitcase was. Despair filled his tired body.

"Jeff, we've done all we can do." Franco put an arm around his shoulder. "The part will be here first thing in the morning. If we have our bags packed, we can be back in Bogota by 10:30 a.m. Thursday."

Jeff kicked the tire of the plane and ran his hand through his hair. "I guess we have no choice."

Jeff woke well before dawn. They had agreed to meet at the car at 5:15, and he wasn't going to be one minute late. And he needed time to pray.

When he returned from a short, dark prayer walk, his watch said five o'clock. Mindy and K.J. were already loading their bags. Franco and David were gulping their morning coffee.

All 20 kids had gotten up to say goodbye. They stood around the car in their pajamas. Laura held one little girl and another clung sleepily to her leg.

Jeff couldn't take his eyes off Laura. He gave her a special hug as he said goodbye. He leaned over to gently wipe away the tear that rolled down her cheek. "I know I'll see you again," he whispered to her. "If not on this earth, then we'll meet in heaven."

Jeff jumped in the back seat of David's car, and

they sped towards the airport. They pulled into the parking lot ten minutes before the flight with the part was due to arrive. Jeff looked up and saw a plane descending. He started shouting, "That's got to be it! And he's ten minutes early."

Everyone clapped each other on the back then ran to Franco's plane. Franco opened the hood, ready to work.

The plane landed and the pilot got out. He shot a thumbs up sign to Franco.

"He's got the part!" Jeff cried.

Everyone surrounded Franco's plane while Franco started to screw the fitting in place. They held their breath.

"Perfect!" Franco proclaimed. "It fits."

It hit Jeff how many lives were hanging on that one little fitting. But when he thought about it, he realized their lives didn't hang on that fitting at all, but on the faithfulness of God. He smiled to himself.

"We'll be ready for takeoff in five minutes," Franco announced.

"Please take your time to make sure everything's okay," Mindy said. "I can't handle another flight like the first one."

Finally, Franco refilled the oil and closed the hood. "We're already fueled up. Everything packed?"

Everybody nodded.

They thanked and hugged David and the pilot who had brought the part.

"Jump inside. Let's go," Franco ordered.

Franco started the engine, and slowly, the propellers began to turn.

From the edge of his seat, Jeff was cheerleading. "Come on, come on."

The engines roared to life, and they all cheered. Franco taxied down the runway and got an okay for takeoff from the controller. The Cessna crawled into the sky as the sun crawled over the horizon.

Mindy kept glancing out the windows. Jeff knew she was checking both engines. But once in the air, they began to relax.

K.J. leaned forward. "Hey! I just remembered I get to do some flying on the way home."

"Oh, brother," Mindy groaned.

"No," K.J. shot back, "your brother already did it. It's my turn."

Franco laughed. "I'll let you take the wheel when we get to cruising altitude."

K.J. made a face at Mindy. "Get some footage of me flying this baby, would ya, Jeff?"

El Dorado Airport was a welcome sight. Jeff hoped Warren and Ricardo would be waiting.

"Hold on," Franco called over his shoulder. "It gets a little windy on the landing."

Jeff knew Mindy didn't want to hear that. He reached for her hand. As usual, K.J. was busy filming.

"I think I see a blue van. Is that Ricardo's?" Jeff asked.

"Yes," Franco said. "You're right. You'll be at the hospital in less than a half hour."

Jeff looked at his watch. It was five minutes before ten.

Chapter 15

The Ticking Clock

Jeff, Mindy, and K.J. quickly thanked their kind friend Franco and said goodbye. He stayed with the plane while they ran as fast as they could to Warren and Ricardo.

"Man, are we glad to see you!" Jeff cried.

"No more than we are," Warren said.

Everyone jumped into the van, and Ricardo sped to the hospital.

"Heard you had a bit of a scare on the ride to Sitka." Warren smiled. "That was close, wasn't it?"

"You wouldn't believe it, Warren." Jeff nodded. "We've had some pretty intense moments."

"You always said you liked adventure," Warren pointed out.

Jeff laughed. "Well, it's never much fun while it's happening. But I do like to look back and remember how the Lord got us out of things." He paused. "What's the latest on Flora?"

"We're still getting calls from Carlos." Warren's voice was heavy. "He says three o'clock today is the final deadline. And I believe him."

"And what about Antonio?" Mindy asked.

"He doesn't want to see anybody but Jeff," Ricardo said. "We're hoping you can open him up."

"Only God can do that," Jeff replied. "I'm going to love him and let God do the rest."

"What if he can't help us find the suitcase?" Mindy fretted. "We only have five hours."

"Somehow, God will save Flora," Ricardo said softly.

As they pulled into the hospital parking lot, Jeff felt his hands shaking. "I don't want to blow it, you guys. There's a lot at stake here. Please keep me in prayer."

They all hurried toward Antonio's room. Roberto, with his arm still bandaged, was waiting outside Antonio's door. He had only been a Christian for a few days, but he and Jeff greeted each other like long-lost brothers. Their smiles and hugs needed no translation.

Ricardo turned to Jeff. "Okay, Jeff. Ready?"

Warren placed his hand on Jeff's shoulder. "We'll be in the waiting room if you need us."

"Okay," Jeff said. "But I'm not going to just run in there and ask about the suitcase. He needs to know that we care."

Ricardo smiled in approval.

Warren gave Jeff a hug. "That's exactly what Jesus would do. Go for it."

Jeff took a deep breath and walked in. He saw Antonio gazing out the hospital window.

"Antonio?" Jeff said gently.

In response, Antonio turned and smiled slightly. Jeff pulled a chair close to his bed.

"How are you doing?" Jeff asked.

"I'm okay, man. I heard you had some problems getting here."

"Yeah. It was scary."

For a moment, there was only silence.

Jeff stirred up his faith and courage. "I heard you wanted to talk to me."

Silence. Finally Antonio spoke. "I've been doing some serious thinking about what you said the other day. I've never heard anybody talk like that. You described my life. And I didn't like it."

Jeff nodded but didn't say anything. He wanted to listen with his heart.

Antonio grimaced as he pulled himself up on the bed. "After you spoke, I wanted to really hurt you. I've learned that the cold truth hurts worse than a knife. I couldn't handle it.

"When the doctor gave me something to help me sleep, I was out for a long time. All I can remember is a dream I had."

Jeff was amazed. This was the most he had ever heard Antonio say.

"I saw myself in the dream," Antonio went on. "I wasn't afraid anymore. I was happy—like you said.

"I hated my dad, man. I wished I could have shot him. And I hated you talking about this heavenly Father. For years, I've hurt anyone who ever talked about a father. I thought all fathers were like mine."

Antonio's eyes fill with tears. "I've never known anything but hate. When you told me you would love me no matter how much I hurt you, I felt angry."

Jeff was speechless. His own eyes were brimming with tears.

"I never thought about Jesus like you said," Antonio continued. "To me, He was a religious nut. I never knew about all the pain and hurt He experienced. *Gamines* can relate. Pain is our language."

Jeff prayed for wisdom. Deep inside, he knew he should keep listening.

"I see now that I've built walls of anger and rage. I did it to protect myself from getting hurt again. But look what it made me into. A street monster, man. A street monster!

"I thought I was tough leading all those kids. Man, they all need what you talked about. They'll be dead in a year or two if you guys don't help them."

Jeff knew it was time to say something. "Maybe you can help, Antonio."

Antonio looked up. "Are you kidding? How can I help? My life is wasted. I'll soon be dead myself."

"Antonio," Jeff said quietly, "I feel the Father's love in this room stronger than I have ever felt it before. He can take away your pain. And your hurt and anger too—if you'll just let it go."

Antonio laughed again, nervously this time. "How?"

"You need to forgive your dad. It's the root of your anger. God has waited a long time for this moment. He's felt your pain for years. Now you need to let it go."

Antonio rolled his eyes. "I was afraid you'd say that. How can I forgive that..."

Jeff just smiled.

"Hey, don't smile at me that way," Antonio said. "I can't handle it."

Jeff waited a moment in silence, praying. "I'll give you time to think about it," he finally said. "It's your decision. It will hurt your pride to let go. But if you do, the Lord will remove the big weight you've been carrying for years."

Antonio's fingers inched across the yellow blanket. He took Jeff's hand and began weeping.

"Can you tell your father you forgive him?" Jeff asked.

"No, I can't. He's dead. He was killed by the drug cartel when I was five." Antonio wept.

Jeff squeezed Antonio's hand in his. "You can forgive him. Just speak words of forgiveness to your dad. The important thing is that you say it, not that he hears it. It's a way of letting go."

Jeff paused. Antonio's face was in anguish. Then, like a torrent of water over a dam, tears and words came tumbling out. "I forgive you, Dad. And I forgive my uncle and everybody else who hurt me."

Antonio started shaking. He wept more and more. Jeff just clung to his hand and cried with him. Antonio's sobbing got stronger until he almost convulsed. Jeff put his arms around Antonio and held him as he prayed.

Then, Antonio was still. Jeff knew peace had come into the room. Jeff squeezed Antonio's hand again and looked into his eyes.

Jeff couldn't believe it. Antonio's face had changed. Free from the poison of bitterness, he looked like an angel.

Jeff wiped his eyes. "Antonio, ask God to come and be your Dad. Ask Jesus into your heart to be your best friend. It'll be forever."

Antonio sobbed as he repeated the words. When he had finished, a huge smile crossed his face. He looked up sheepishly. "I need to tell you something. The other day when I was so angry, I wanted to hurt you. And I found a way."

Jeff's eyes grew bigger as Antonio went on. "After you gave us money on the street that day, my friends and I followed you home. I knew where you were staying. When I got mad at you, I took some stuff from the house."

Jeff couldn't believe his ears. "Did you take a suitcase, Antonio?"

"Yes. I'm sorry. Stealing was the only life I knew."

Jeff hesitated before going on. "Antonio, when we came here today, the most important thing was you. But that suitcase is very important too. If we get it back, it'll save somebody's life."

Jeff waited, holding his breath. Then he quickly

glanced at his watch. He couldn't believe it was noon.

"I was going to sell it," Antonio continued. "But for some reason I didn't. It's stashed in an abandoned building. I can tell you how to find it. I hope the other kids haven't taken it."

Jeff told Antonio about Flora's kidnapping and the importance of finding the suitcase. Then he stuck his head out the door and called to Ricardo. When he came in, Antonio told him exactly where to find the suitcase.

Jeff wanted to say one more thing. "I promise I'll be back. We'll arrange for you to have a new home at the center. You'll be helping hundreds of kids before long."

"I hope so," Antonio said. "You'd better hurry."

Jeff and Ricardo ran to the waiting room. They told everybody what had happened.

"Carlos gave me a number to call," Ricardo said. "I'll go find a phone. You guys pray."

Jeff and the others waited. The timing was tight, and Jeff could almost hear a ticking clock in his head. It made him jumpy.

Finally, Ricardo ran back from the phone. "Carlos told me to get the suitcase and meet him in the park—the one we were at during the earthquake. He wants the suitcase in a cardboard box. He'll tell us where to find Flora after he has it. Let's go."

"I hope those kids didn't take it," Mindy muttered.

Ricardo stopped at the center to pick up a cardboard box. Then they rushed down a back alley to the old building. It had been abandoned for years and served as a hiding place for street kids.

Jeff, Mindy, K.J., and Warren followed Ricardo. He looked like he knew exactly where to go.

Street kids peeked out of their dark hiding places as they ran by. Ricardo stopped behind a broken-down wall. He pawed around behind it for a moment. Then he looked up.

"It's not here!"

Chapter 16

Prime Time

It's got to be!" Jeff exclaimed.

Ricardo shoved old boxes out of the way. "Quick! Help me find it."

They searched frantically.

"It's hopeless." Mindy was in tears.

"What time is it?" K.J. asked.

Jeff looked at his watch. "Almost two."

A group of scruffy kids gathered around. Jeff recognized them as Antonio's gang. The oldest one stepped forward. He looked up at Jeff and muttered something.

"What did he say, Ricardo?" Jeff tried to control his panic.

"He says he has what we're looking for. Before Antonio was shot, he told him we might come looking for it."

"Did he tell you where it is?" Mindy cried.

"He heard we've been taking care of Antonio," Ricardo replied, "so he's willing to lead us to it."

They followed the band of kids around the back side of the building and knelt behind some trash cans. Leaning over, Jeff spotted a patch of color—the burgundy suitcase!

The boy pulled it out and handed it to Ricardo with a grin.

"What's he saying?" Jeff wanted to know.

"He moved it so no one else could steal it."

Like a shot, Ricardo was off to the park. He yelled over his shoulder as he went, "Meet you at the center! Pray!"

Jeff hugged Flora tightly. "I'm glad you're okay."

Everyone at the center wept for joy, taking turns hugging her. Then Flora and Ricardo hugged—but this hug lasted much longer than the others. Flora was glowing when she turned to face everyone.

"What do you think, Flora?" Ricardo asked, staring into her eyes. "Should we tell them?"

She nodded with an embarrassed grin.

"Flora and I have been praying about marriage for months," Ricardo began. "We had vowed to stay apart for a month to seek the Lord's will. Then she was kidnapped. Being apart made every minute torture for both of us."

Flora blushed as he took her hand. Tears welled up in Ricardo's eyes and a smile filled his face. "We're getting married in the spring."

Jeff, Mindy, K.J., and Warren smothered the happy couple in hugs and congratulations.

Later, at the ICC house, K.J. looked gloomy.

"What's wrong?" Jeff asked.

"It's not fair."

"What's not fair? Are you bummed Flora is marrying Ricardo?" Mindy teased.

"No, I'm not," K.J. flung back, although his face turned a bright red. "It's just that those drug dealers got off totally free. They got the suitcase and the money. They must be laughing."

Ricardo grinned. "K.J., I have a confession. I found a piece of paper in the suitcase. It was what the drug cartel was really after."

"What was on the paper?" Mindy asked.

"The names of their connections in the drug cartel." A sneaky grin crossed Ricardo's face. "I copied the names on the list. I'll be giving it to a law enforcement officer I know. He hates crime and can be trusted. One by one, everyone on the list will get busted over the next few months."

Everyone cheered and laughed out loud.

At the Los Angeles television studio, The Reel Kids Club waited. Their video had just been aired on prime time.

Jeff scanned the rows of people answering the phones. Every operator was busy.

"Are you sure you didn't have any professional help with this video?" the producer standing next to him teased. "We've never had such an immediate response to a program before. You did a wonderful job. I expect big things from you guys in the future."

Jeff smiled at K.J. and Mindy. Warren puffed up his chest and nodded with satisfaction.

The producer smiled, handing Jeff a taped copy of the show. "I think your friends in Colombia will be helping kids for a long time to come."

Jeff looked heavenward, smiling.